THE HAUNTING OF WILLOW CREEK

A HOPEFUL HORROR NOVEL

SARA CROCOLL SMITH

FUN, FICTION, FANDOM

The Haunting of Willow Creek
A Hopeful Horror Novel

Cover design by Janet Linton

Editing by C.B. Calsing

Disability sensitivity reading by Erin Perkins

ISBN 978-1-956546-13-2 (ebook)

ISBN 978-1-956546-14-9 (paperback)

ISBN 978-1-956546-15-6 (hardcover)

ISBN 978-1-956546-16-3 (large print)

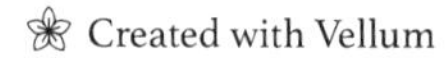
Created with Vellum

To friendship. Like flowers that grow in the same garden. Magnificent, unique, all reaching toward the light together.

FREE SHORT STORY

You can't escape its grasp...

Concerned about her mother's unsettling phone calls, Samantha returns home from abroad to find the curtains drawn and the windows nailed shut.

Is dementia causing her mother's strange behavior or something much more sinister?

Claustrophobic humidity... creeping ivy... dark secrets...

Samantha's been the perfect daughter her entire life. As she uncovers what lies at the heart of her childhood home, she'll never be the same again.

Visit SaraCrocollSmith.com/Ivy to get the free short story "The Strangle of Ivy."

1

Billows of ruddy dust flared under the tires of Birdie Montgomery's sedan as the pothole-filled road shifted to uneven gravel. The parched Georgian clay wrinkled under the unforgiving summer sun, cracks splitting the land like the lightning it longed for during the drought-filled weeks of August.

As Birdie left the southernmost back roads of the state, only a small buckshot sign marked Keep Out signaled her entrance onto the private property. She rubbed her sweaty hands on her yellow dress dotted with daisies, then turned down the volume on the increasingly static-laden country radio station.

With a renewed grip on the steering wheel, she slowed the vehicle over the bumpy drive. All evidence of civilization fell away, aside from the rough road she focused on navigating and the brittle, overgrown flora lining the path ahead.

A roundabout punctuated the end of the drive. Birdie decided to park before circling around and walk the short rest of the way to take in her new temporary place of residence.

Sullen willow trees blocked her view of Willow Creek Mansion, the tips of the branches browning as if they'd been dipped in rust. She stepped out of the car and straightened her dress, her dark brown boots already caking with the fine cinnamon dust.

Birdie walked around to the other side of the car, the ebbing ticks of her engine settling down, melding into the soft hush of a slight breeze through the grass. Everything she owned was either crammed in the back seat or the tiny trunk of her car. She'd left behind a cookie-cutter studio apartment, a couple of dead plants, and an unsatisfying waitress job in Atlanta when she found out she'd been awarded the Willa Cromwell Artists of Perception Grant.

The gilding on the acceptance letter was so thrilling and excessive, it'd made her think of Willy Wonka's golden ticket. It was a brand-new grant: offered room and board at a mansion in southern Georgia, utilities, and even a small stipend that was slightly better than the job she'd quit to come here. With openings for only five artists of different disciplines, she didn't think that she'd snag the sole visual artist spot. But here she was.

Lifting her hand to shield her eyes from the sun, she looked around. So far, it wasn't quite the splendor she'd imagined. Yet nothing was going to stop her from delivering a stellar photographic series based on the eponymous willows of the area at the end of her residency.

Perhaps she just needed to look at the area from a different angle.

Through the open passenger-side window, Birdie retrieved her camera. She brought it up to her right eye and cradled its long lens. The tension in her shoulders eased as she viewed her surroundings through the eye of the camera.

Birdie's boots crunched as she left the gravel drive to wander into knee-high grasses. She ignored the urge to itch where the grass tickled her calves and instead focused the camera on some craggy bark on a nearby tree. Clinging to the bark like a honey-colored, glass-blown bug was the hunchback of a cicada shell, long vacated.

She tucked the strap of the camera over her neck and let it hang as she leaned forward to touch the shell. It fell to the ground to join a pile of dozens of its brethren gathered in a clumped ring around the base of the tree.

Cicada season had ended quite a few weeks ago, but the remnants lingered. She snapped a few more pictures, focusing on the split back of another clinging shell where the previous occupant had left behind its former self. She marveled at the life cycle of a cicada: born in the tree canopy, plummet to the ground, travel through the roots, feed there for a decade or two, then rise again to be born anew. Even though she was born and raised in Georgia, the natural beauty of the land never failed to offer new inspiration for her photos.

Birdie marched toward the roundabout, determined to take in more of the aura of the estate and finally see the mansion, before unloading her car. As she came around the bend, Willow Creek Mansion revealed its face through the countless old willow trees at last.

The mansion smirked at her from within its rare shade and seclusion from the late summer heat. Though all the willows, with aging moss adorning their shoulders like macabre feather boas, appeared to lean away from the house, their sheer multitudes accumulated shadows on the stirring giant.

On her slow procession closer, Birdie examined its details through her zoom lens. The mansion was wide, with two stories, each with floor-to-ceiling windows indicative of the high ceilings that must lay inside. Four broad pillars supported the overhanging roof, creating a cavernous porch. Lazy wicker fans twirled over deep-back chairs, their cream paint peeling only slightly.

Birdie climbed the first step up the porch toward the great double doors which were painted pale green. To the right of the doors, on the uneven porch floor, lay a pile of dead willow branches as high as her waist. She raised her eyebrows, but her attention was drawn toward a tall figure to the left covered in a yellowing tablecloth. Her heart sped in her chest, unsure what to make of it.

Unwilling to venture farther onto the porch, she turned into the blinding sunlight bathing the front yard and let it beam down warmly on her face. Several cars were already parked in the drive. She held her breath and listened for signs of any of the other artists.

Nearby, grasshoppers made their spring and chirp noises, flinging into the air like flipped coins in the overgrown grass. Cocking her head, she thought she heard voices drifting through an open window of the mansion. Before she could investigate, something metallic winked at her from the distance through the hanging arms of the willow trees.

Peering through her camera, she tracked a beat-up muscle car barreling toward the house. Loud folk music blared from the speakers, a mix of blues and southern soul. The driver whisked the car up the drive and slammed on their brakes to park directly in front of Birdie.

The driver-side door swung open, and out stepped a confident woman in a flowy, bohemian dress that highlighted her long legs. She wore a wide brim hat that covered her face, revealing only the untamed chestnut-colored hair that cascaded down her back. With a flourish that indicated the music she'd since turned off still rang out in her head, the woman belted the lyrics beautifully while she retrieved a long-necked black guitar case from the backseat.

Birdie's mouth went dry, and she swallowed hard. She knew that accepting this grant, to stay here for three months at Willow Creek Mansion, unfortunately also meant she had to share the space with four other artists.

Other artists could be the absolute worst. The ones she'd encountered were so into themselves, into their own worlds, they often lost sight of the people around them. But she figured a mansion had to be *huge*, right? She could get through three months with other people in a big enough place.

As the woman approached her—shoulders back, slipping off her hat and pressing it to her breast with a small bow—Birdie chewed on her lip and tried not to swear. She never understood how people could prop themselves up like that, like cocky little birds strutting about. The presence and audacity it took to consume that much space, especially when meeting a stranger—

"Hello!" The woman had emerald-green eyes and freckles that lined the bridge of her nose and cheeks. Her smile was wry as she spoke. "I'm Dodge Dawson. Who might you be?"

Birdie cleared her throat and held out her hand. "Birdie Montgomery. Nice to meet you."

Dodge shrugged, gesturing to her guitar case in one hand and the hat in the other. Birdie crossed her arms, hugging her camera to her stomach.

Dodge tilted her head slightly and Birdie felt the woman eye her with amusement. "Pleasure's all mine, love. You a photographer?"

Birdie nodded.

Dodge started up the stairs toward the door. Birdie studied the ornate stitching on her ankle high cowboy boots. "Folk musician. As if it was some great mystery." She chuckled and stooped to set her guitar case down on the porch, then wrinkled her nose. "Chef must be here. Can't ya smell it?"

Birdie sniffed the air and a sweetness wafted by. Her stomach rumbled in response. She wasn't sure how she missed that before. There was a lot to take in here. "Yeah. Guess you're right."

Dodge tipped her head toward the door. "You go in yet?"

Birdie opened her mouth, then closed it and shook her head.

"Seems like a heck of a weird place." Dodge wiggled her eyebrows and clapped her hands together. "Can't wait to see what's inside. Gonna be great inspiration for new songs. I've been in a bit of a rut lately. This residency will really help get my butt in gear."

Dodge rapped on the door, three confident knocks. After a couple of seconds of silence, Birdie fiddling with the camera's lens, Dodge blew a big puff of air upward, her hair ruffling under its force. "Oh, heck. Let's just get on in there."

Birdie looked left and right, frowning at the

sheet-covered figure that didn't seem to bother Dodge at all. "Are you sure we should—"

Dodge waved her forward. "Come on, come on."

Birdie stepped closer as the door creaked open. Her toe caught on an uneven porch board, spilling her toward the very figure she'd wanted to avoid. Scrambling, she grabbed onto the sheet and toppled over, letting out a small shriek as she came face to face with a woven, gnarled wooden face. Its rictus grin and hollow eyes stared at her as she crab walked away until she backed against one of the porch pillars.

Heavy boots stomped toward her, rattling the boards like an angry earthquake underneath her palms. A broad man with a handle-bar mustache crossed his arms over his white tank top, huge biceps on full display. He scowled down at her. "My sculpture was covered for a reason. It isn't done yet. Now you've gone and ruined the process. I'll have to start all over again."

"Sculpture?" Birdie stammered.

She looked at the terrifying figure again and realized that it was composed of willow branches woven together with other various bits of nature and organic materials. It reminded her of how birds create their nests out of anything they can find. She wasn't sure why anyone would want to make such a horrifying sculpture but was smart enough to keep her mouth shut.

The man turned his back on them and disappeared into the house. Dodge came over to Birdie, stifling a giggle with her hand before offering it to help Birdie onto her feet. "I guess that's our sculptor. What an odd duck. He's gonna be a riot."

Dodge grabbed her guitar case and crossed the

threshold. She glanced back over her shoulder at Birdie. “Come on in, love.” She beckoned her before disappearing as well.

Birdie breathed hard for a moment, unable to break eye contact with the empty sockets of the sculpture’s eyes. She hurried over, grabbed the sheet, and dashed it on top of the hideous face. She kicked her toe at the uneven board, noticing a tree root had pushed it out of place. Keeping nature from completely taking over an estate like this must be quite the feat.

Taking one last view of the sun-soaked front yard and drive, the light breeze again whispering through the grass, Birdie entered Willow Creek Mansion.

2

Birdie paused in the mansion's foyer, then shut the door behind her. Her hand lingered on the taut, cream curtains that shaded the wavy, aged glass of the double doors. She sighed and closed her eyes. Behind her, the sculptor's heavy boots carried him and his anger upstairs. A light clanging of pots and utensils echoed from down the hall, followed by laughter. Tension rose in her shoulders as the fullness of the house pressed against her.

A finger tapped her on the back, and she flinched. Birdie turned around and was greeted by a charming man, only slightly taller than herself, dressed elegantly in a beige, button-down shirt, an evergreen vest, and matching slacks. She stared at his gleaming brown dress shoes while he spoke.

"You all right there, honey?" He reached out and grabbed her hands, holding them in his, reminding her of how her grandmother would do so when Birdie was younger. She raised her eyebrows, part of her wanting to resist the overly friendly gesture, part of her wanting to confide in him. "You look like you've seen a ghost."

Birdie glanced back at the door. "I knocked over

the sculpture. I think he's mad at me." Her cheeks flushed hot.

The man released her hands, shaking one of his like he was shooing a fly. "Don't you mind that grumpy ol' sculptor. Tom will get over it."

"Hey, you two. Drinks are ready." A woman called from the kitchen with a hint of a Spanish accent. Birdie only caught a brief glimpse of her: white coat, dark hair pulled back in a ponytail. The chef.

The man at Birdie's side offered her the crook of his arm, and she took it. "I'm Marcel Owen, by the way. Orator, poet, elocutionist of the greatest magnitude." Marcel swept his free arm out grandly and led her down the hall to the kitchen. He leaned close to whisper in her ear. "Between you and me, you did us all a favor. That sculpture was *hideous*."

Birdie stifled a laugh. They entered a grand kitchen with high ceilings dripping in intricate molding. The cream paint had a grubby patina that brought charm and character to the space. A long white-and-gray marbled counter sectioned off the cooking area from the row of wicker bar stools where Dodge perched. A stout dining table bathed in sunlight by the windows. Gauzy curtains danced softly in the light cross flow of air. Over the table, a wheel-shaped bronze chandelier hung with half-melted candles punctuating the spokes. Birdie imagined come night, when it was lit, the chandelier would be dazzling.

The chef worked at the counter, various bottles and condiments next to two large glass pitchers. She wiped a hand on her apron and held it out. "Adriana Martinez. Culinary artist." Her smile was warm. Her amber eyes had a bright intellect about them that Birdie found intimidating.

Realizing she still held Marcel's arm, she unhooked herself from him and raised on her tiptoes to shake Adriana's hand over the counter. "I'm Birdie Montgomery." She lifted her camera gingerly. "Photographer."

Marcel pulled out a chair for her and slid into the one next to Dodge. "Birdie. What a delightful name."

She played with her camera strap, then took her seat. Usually she could tell when someone was being sarcastic about her name, but Marcel's statement sounded genuine. "Thanks. It's short for Beatrice. But everyone's called me Birdie since I was little, and it just stuck."

He patted her hand. "It suits you. You and your bird's-eye view of the world with that camera. Can't wait to see what pictures you take out here."

Birdie caught Dodge's eye, who nodded with a slight smirk. "There's certainly a lot of good subject matter out here for a visual medium like yours."

Marcel threw his hands up in the air. "Darling Adriana, you've been teasing us for far too long. Look at this hand." He tapped a finger on his empty palm. "This poor thing deserves to be holding a champagne flute, if I do say so myself."

Adriana laughed. "*Sí, sí.* Hold your horses." She lined up a few champagne flutes and tumblers. One pitcher held an orange-red liquid and the other a golden-hued concoction. "Marcel, I assume you'd like to try one of my blood orange mimosas?"

He nodded.

Dodge added, "Put me down for one too, please."

Adriana looked to Birdie.

"No, thank you."

Adriana poured three glasses of mimosas, garnishing them with fresh thyme and a blood orange slice. As she served one each to Dodge and Marcel, she grinned. “You know, Birdie, I’m actually glad you don’t want one.” Adriana sipped from her own glass, closing her eyes and sighing with satisfaction. “Don’t get me wrong, they’re delicious.”

“Damn right, honey,” Marcel said. Dodge nodded in agreement.

Adriana pulled a tumbler close. Then she used a slender glass stirrer in the other pitcher. Birdie watched as the golden liquid sloshed inside. “But it’s not a proper summer day in Georgia without some sweet tea. Will you try my new recipe and tell me how it came out?”

Cradling the glass in her hands, Birdie took a tentative taste. The sweetness glided across her tongue, smooth and comforting. It cooled her from the inside, soothing the August heat she had long since grown accustomed to. She paused and looked up at Adriana. “That’s the best cup of sweet tea I’ve ever had,” Birdie said. “My grandmother’s recipe goes back generations in Georgia, and this blows it out of the water.” She again allowed herself a smile, despite her efforts to remain distanced from them. Maybe the stay wouldn’t be so bad after all. “What’s your secret?”

Hands on her hips, Adriana beamed. “I knew I was onto something special.” She sorted through the condiments and held up a tiny, glass bee-shaped jar labeled *Orchard Hill Honey*. “I got this on a trek to upstate New York. A little apple orchard off the main road. I think I’m going to source it from them and make it part of my signature dessert dish when I open my restaurant.”

"Restaurant?" Birdie said, taking another drink. It tasted like home.

"Sí. This residency is my opportunity to save up the rest of the money I need while also refining my menu." Adriana checked her watch. "Now that we're all here, I think it's the perfect night for my fancy s'mores. We can do it out by the creek. Tom's been here a week already and set up a fire pit out there."

"How long have you two been here?" Dodge asked.

"Just since the weekend, couple of days," Adriana said. "How about this? I'll pack up the picnic basket with everything we need. While I do that, Marcel, can you help show them around to their rooms? You two should have enough time to bring in your things and settle before we need to head out. I'll whip up some light snacks you can grab in the meantime for dinner. You'll want to keep your appetite for these s'mores." She whirled with confidence and started pulling items out of the cabinets. "Meet you on the porch at eight o'clock. Okay?"

Marcel stood, held his mimosa above his head, and marched toward the foyer. "There's nothing I'd love more than to be your tour guide through Willow Creek Mansion. You've yet to properly meet the lady of the house."

"*Marcel.*" Adriana's voice sounded stern as she set her ingredients next to an oversized picnic basket. "Don't scare them. It's not that bad."

In a graceful half turn, he shot her side-eye. "If this mimosa wasn't so good, I'd question your taste. Because what is happening upstairs is a decorative tragedy that should be burned." Marcel crooked two fingers at Dodge and Birdie, each of whom carried their drinks with them. "Follow me, lovely ladies."

After moving through the foyer, Marcel led them up a wide, winding staircase to the second floor. Birdie hadn't paid much attention to the area when she'd entered the mansion, distracted by what happened with the sculpture and meeting everyone. Now, she didn't know how she'd missed it. Marcel paused on the landing halfway up, and she felt him taking in their reactions.

Covering every inch of the walls were portraits. These, however, were not the aging oil paintings of a typical southern Georgia mansion, gaudy and gathering dust. These were portraits crafted from all types of media, varying widely in shape, size, color, texture—portraits of the same person, over and over again, to a dizzying degree. Her face was plain. Hundreds of dull eyes peered at Birdie from every angle. A small, displeased mouth sat underneath an unremarkable nose. Mousy brown hair hung limply at her shoulders. No matter how the woman was depicted—whether it be collage, mixed media, watercolor, charcoal drawing, even stained glass—nothing kept her from being forgettable and ordinary.

Birdie held her breath under their collective, inanimate gaze. Dodge sidestepped closer to Birdie, as if in solidarity. Marcel, never seeming at a loss for words, did not take his moment to boast. Instead he put his hand to his chest with a disapproving glance upward, then carried on up the rest of the stairs while they followed.

Only once they were in the upstairs hall and past the portraits did Birdie feel the pressure on her sternum ease and she could breathe again. "What was that?" she asked, a little breathless.

Marcel wrapped an arm around her shoulder, his carefree demeanor betrayed by lines of tension between his brows. "That was Willa Cromwell. Our deceased benefactress and ever-watchful host."

"Good golly." Dodge wandered farther down the hall. "That's some next-level narcissism."

"Indeed," Marcel said. "An interior design crime of epic proportions."

"Who made all of these?" Birdie approached the railing and set her drink down on an end table.

Marcel joined her and leaned against the railing, his back to the stairwell gallery. "Willa commissioned these portraits from various artists during her lifetime."

Birdie raised her camera, then zoomed in on a portrait in the farthest corner of the entryway ceiling. Shrouded in shadow, Willa's sallow complexion glinted in the faint light that dared illuminate its surface. Birdie squinted and attempted to discern the artistic medium used to create the portrait. It almost looked to Birdie like the enamel of—

She let out a small yelp and dropped her camera, which banged softly against her chest and settled at the end of the strap. The blood drained from her face as she gripped the banister, looking down hard at the floor.

"What's wrong?" Marcel asked.

A gentle hand turned her around, then cupped Birdie's cheek. "You look pale." Birdie expected Marcel but was surprised by Dodge's concern. "Marcel, why don't you show us to our rooms? Perhaps Birdie can lie down a while. The heat of this day could get the better of anyone."

"Of course." Marcel led them down the hall. It was expansive. Birdie thought if she spread her arms out, she'd never be able to touch both walls at once. She counted maybe five doors on each side. Marcel pointed as they walked. "This is my room. Adriana's. Tom's."

Dodge trailed closely next to Birdie and whispered. "What did you see?"

"What?" Something about Dodge made Birdie uneasy: a woman who looked like she did and knew it. Birdie didn't have a history of those type of women being good friends. Usually any play at genuine friendship somehow got mangled, betrayed. The back of Birdie's neck tickled with a nervous sensation, and she rubbed at it.

Dodge leaned closer, observing Birdie, and then set her lips in a line, nodding. "Okay. You don't have to tell me if you don't want to."

Birdie shrugged her off. There was no way she could tell Dodge what she thought she saw up there. She may not be the best at getting to know people and small talk, but she sure as heck knew it didn't involve mentioning human teeth. Besides, she was probably wrong. It was likely something obvious, something like beads or pebbles. She worked in photographs, not mixed media.

In the middle of the hall, an elaborately carved double door dwarfed the other relatively plain, wood-paneled doors. Marcel stopped and raised his half-empty champagne flute in a toast. "This is Willa's room." He jiggled the handle, then pouted. "It's locked. Apparently, we're not allowed in. Something about not disturbing the artifacts and history, blah, blah, blah." He waved his glass, beckoning them onward. "I'll figure out how to pick the lock at some point. We deserve to know more about the woman who had such benevolent foresight as to set up a grant for fifty years after her death. She's just begging to be unearthed, darlings."

Dodge laughed. "I actually know a thing or two about lock picking."

Marcel dropped back and looped arms with Dodge. "Ooh, honey, I do love a colorful past. Tell me more."

Birdie frowned. "Maybe we should leave it alone." But her words didn't carry over the conspiring laughter of the other two artists in front of her.

3

Birdie found herself alone on the front porch. Her watch told her it was five past eight. She avoided the overturned sculpture, still laying on the porch boards covered by the cloth like a body at a crime scene, thankful she hadn't encountered Tom again since earlier. The pile of old willow branches by the door had tumbled over half of the discarded creation. If she wasn't so creeped out by it, her instincts to tidy up might've taken over.

Five more minutes passed. At first, she sat on the wicker bench. Too antsy to sit long, she got up. She popped her head back inside the doors and flicked on the porch lights. Inside, she heard what she assumed was Adriana making final preparations in the kitchen. From upstairs came a beautiful voice, singing a folk song she'd never heard before, a song about a meadow siren. Birdie, captivated, listened as Dodge paused and resang the last line. She realized Dodge was writing the lyrics as she sang. It was an original piece.

Marcel joined in, a piercing falsetto that made Birdie flinch. Then Marcel and Dodge both broke off singing and chattered while they presumably finished getting ready. Not wanting to come off as uptight while waiting on them, Birdie slipped back outside to wait.

The sun disappeared beneath the horizon, raking its ruddy fingers through the willow leaves of the trees in the front yard. Toads croaked as the day darkened. She could still taste the sweetness of Adriana's tea on her tongue, and her stomach rumbled in anticipation of what "fancy s'mores" made by Adriana might entail. Having a culinary artist as one of the residents during their stay might not turn out to be such a bad thing. Birdie never took to cooking much herself, so anything Adriana made would be a treat. If Adriana's tea were any notion, she definitely had talent.

As she turned to see if Adriana needed any assistance and possibly help herself to some more of the tea, Dodge opened the door, giggling. "Marcel, hurry up!"

"Hold onto your britches, darling. I'm setting a *mood*," Marcel hollered back from the top of the stairs.

Dodge rolled her eyes in a show for Birdie. "I can't wait to see what that means." She flopped down on the wicker bench, her cowboy boots swaying over the armrest. Dodge had changed into slim riding pants with a bloused black shirt and fresh lipstick. Birdie had opted for high rise jeans, hiking boots, and a tank top. She couldn't help but compare herself to Dodge's edgier style.

Reaching for her camera, she remembered she left it in her room. She didn't think it was likely she'd take many pictures after dark, yet she felt naked without it.

Dodge made room on the bench and patted the

seat next to her. "He's going to be at least a few minutes. Come, sit, relax."

After Marcel had shown them to their room, Birdie was less than thrilled to find out her room was adjoined with Dodge's through a shared bathroom. Birdie had hidden her discomfort since Dodge seemed all too at home with the arrangement and Birdie didn't want to come off unnecessarily rude.

Birdie nodded and sat on the bench. She leaned against the backrest yet remained stiff as if her body rejected Dodge's command to relax.

They listened to the sounds of the awakening night together. Birdie watched the last of the sunlight disappear, leaving only streaks of maroon to outline the few clouds in the sky. Night was never her favorite time. She much preferred the natural light of day when she could clearly see her surroundings.

Next to her, Dodge rested her head back on the bench, eyes closed, with a pleasant smile on her face.

Birdie cleared her throat. "Was that your song?"

"Hmmm?" Dodge laced her fingers over her own chest.

"You were singing upstairs." Birdie played with a loop on her jeans. "It was beautiful."

Dodge opened her eyes, peering up at Birdie. "Thank you, love. It's a little something new I've been noodling with."

The door creaked open, startling Birdie. Dodge sat up. Tom, in the same outfit of heavy boots and white muscle tank, joined them on the porch. He didn't spare a glance at his sculpture, just grunted a greeting at them as he moved to lean against a nearby pillar, crossing his arms in front of his chest.

"Hiya," Dodge said.

Sweat moistened Birdie's palms. Toppling and unveiling his sculpture had been an accident, but she couldn't stand the tension of starting off on the wrong foot with one of the four people she had to share the mansion with for a couple of months. She may not be as quirky about her artistic methods; however she could be particular in ways she didn't realize and should make an effort to respect someone else's process.

Birdie rose from the bench and approached Tom. He didn't look at her as she spoke. "Tom? I'm really sorry about earlier."

His mustache twitched. He shifted his weight and unfurled his biceps. "Don't worry about it." Then Tom reached into one of the large cargo pockets on his pants and withdrew two wooden items about the length of a ruler. He handed one to Birdie and the other to Dodge. "Here. I made these for you."

Birdie examined it. The craftsmanship spoke of exquisite talent. She slowly spread open the hand fan, admiring the composite woven and carved materials. Perched on the end of the handle sat a delicate wooden bird.

Next to her, Dodge whipped hers open. "This is amazing. I love the adorable rabbit on mine."

Tom made eye contact with Birdie for a brief moment before breaking away again. "I thought they might be handy in this heat."

Birdie smiled. She considered that sometimes big men forgot how imposing they could be. Now that she'd had a slightly longer interaction with

Tom, she spotted some of the socially anxious traits she herself dealt with. The tightness in her neck and shoulders abated. If he spent all afternoon making their gifts to make up to them, that was certainly something.

"Thank you." She fanned herself. "It really does help."

The door opened, and Adriana came out, an enormous picnic basket cradled effortlessly in the crook of her arm. She held the door for Marcel, who stepped onto the porch with flair and bowed.

"That's an awfully pretty outfit, Marcel. I love this scarf." Dodge moved closer and touched the rose-colored silk gathered at his neck.

He tipped an imaginary hat at her. "Thank you, my dear. But it's not a scarf; it's a *cravat*. The specificity of words is best not forgotten, as words are all we have to separate ourselves from the beasts." Marcel winked playfully at Birdie, smoothing the front of his vest, this one a stunning teal and gold jacquard. "I wanted to feel like a proper Southern gentleman for our social excursion this evening. I might even treat you to a lovely soliloquy tonight."

Tom kicked off the pillar and started cleaning up the spilled willow branches that had fallen over his covered sculpture. "You're overdressed. We're walking in the woods along the creek, not going to a party."

Marcel straightened and chuckled. "Honey, everywhere I go is a party."

Dodge pointed to the branches in Tom's arms. "I saw those earlier. What're they for?"

"They were hanging over every door in the mansion when we got here," Adriana said. She reached her hand in the basket and withdrew several flashlights, handing one to each of them.

"I took them down, the crumbly old things." Marcel descended the porch steps. "They completely ruined the aesthetic. Gave it hillbilly hell vibes and did nothing for the stately, if not slightly ruinous, beauty of the place."

Dodge followed Marcel to the front yard. Birdie hung back near Tom, who'd since repiled the branches in a better position against the wall. "I feel like I've seen that done before in other parts of Georgia." Birdie hesitated. "Don't you think someone put them there for a reason?"

Marcel pressed the back of his hand to his forehead in a mock faint. "My, my, little bird of Georgia. Are we a superstitious one?"

Tom squatted and lifted his sheet-covered sculpture in his arms. "I told him not to do it," he mumbled under his breath.

Once the rest of them joined Marcel and Dodge in the yard, a couple of them flicked on their flashlights and they began walking along a faintly worn path that wove around the side of the house. Their flashlights danced, search lights in the dark, bright and narrow, casting shifting shadows. Birdie wrapped her arms around herself, goose bumps rising despite the warm evening.

Birdie was thankful none of them could see the scowl on her face. She'd grown to like Marcel from the one-on-one interaction she'd had with him. Yet, his need to perform in front of the others made him careless about taking the jests too far. It touched a nerve in her that she thought she'd left behind since spending a number of years living in Atlanta. But the southern backwoods never truly leave a person, does it?

Marcel continued without waiting for an answer. "You're in the right place for it, honey."

"Why's that?" Dodge asked. Something in her tone made Birdie look over at her. She sounded magnitudes less playful than before. Was she defending Birdie?

Adriana spoke back over her shoulder at them. "I asked about the branches when I went into town for groceries yesterday. They told me branches hung over a threshold are meant to protect against *brujas*."

Marcel walked ahead, leading the way. "*Witches.*" He let loose a cheerful cackle that echoed in the night as they rounded the back of the property and entered plunging darkness.

4

Fireflies levitated on the close humidity of the night air. Birdie trudged through the knee-high grass near the back of the pack. Marcel and Adriana chatted at the front of the group, followed closely by Dodge. Behind Birdie, she heard Tom's footfalls carrying him and his sculpture. The rear of the mansion was in a fair amount of disarray compared to the front. While the signs of time ravaging the building had been evident via peeling, discolored paint, and uneven floorboards, nature had taken even more of a toll in the backyard. Birdie couldn't make out everything, noting she'd like to explore more in the daylight, but several pieces of siding were loose or had fallen.

At the very edge of the property, sitting like a hunchback in the dark, a rotting shed with a severe lean was the last thing they passed before the trail curved and molded itself along the creek side.

Birdie listened with interest to the water trickling nearby. By the sliver of moonlight, the creek glistened blue-gray at its lowest points. She guessed it was about fifteen feet across when the water level was normal, no telling how deep it'd be when the rains finally relieved them of the drought. Willows lined the path such that the group traveled underneath and at times through their drooping arms.

A high-pitched screech sounded nearby. Adriana skidded to a stop, dropping the picnic basket. Birdie stooped to help her collect the fallen items, glad that it gave her an excuse to huddle near someone.

"What was that?" Marcel asked, his voice loud as if it alone could fend off any danger.

"Shhh," said Tom. "Listen."

Again they heard the frightening scream. Another answering call came from across the creek.

Dodge spoke softly. "Sounds like a woman."

"No." Marcel shone his flashlight on Tom as Tom shook his head, pensive, brows serious. "Those are red foxes." He frowned, which was all the more deeply emphasized by his large mustache. Tom cocked his head, they all heard the calls again, this time farther ahead. "It's odd though. Mating season is earlier in the year. They shouldn't be active this late in August."

Birdie helped Adriana stand. Marcel pointed the flashlight down the path and shook out his shoulders. "Well, okay then. Mother Nature is apparently showing me who's boss at setting a spooky mood."

Dodge laughed, and Adriana joined her. Birdie couldn't help but smile, though she imagined a disapproving look from Tom in the dark. At least a decade had passed since she'd heard foxes scream in the night. She hadn't missed it.

After a few more minutes of walking, Adriana paused. "Tom, how much farther?"

"Just beyond the brush ahead. It'll open into a

clearing," he called to her. "You can't miss the Weeping Willow."

Birdie could hear the capital letters in Tom's voice. "What's *the* Weeping Willow?" she asked. They continued forward. Birdie, thankful she chose hiking boots for the occasion, stepped over the brush. She took the hand Dodge offered to clear the last high bit of tangled weeds.

"Yeah," Dodge said. "This whole place is nothing but weepin' willows, far as the eye can see."

"You'll see." Tom lifted his sculpture overhead as he trudged through the brush on his long legs like it was nothing. "Turn around."

Birdie did as she was instructed. Adriana and Marcel already faced the imposing figure, a silhouetted giant backlit by weak moonlight. Dodge let out a low whistle as she and Birdie joined them. Adriana's mouth hung open slightly while Marcel's was firmly shut, though Birdie could tell by the gleam in his eyes he was conjuring something witty to say.

Wind rustled through the leaves, a soft caress on Birdie's shoulder, the dry sounds they made a whisper that prickled her senses. Unthinking, drawn to the tree, she raised her flashlight on its face. Her light ran over a fire pit, five chairs, and a small folding table huddled in the shadow of the Weeping Willow before finally illuminating the tree itself.

All other willows in the area paled in comparison. Many of the others had taken on an amber hue under the withering hand of the August drought. Their leaves brittle, their branches frail, each one blending into another, arms intertwined, a sea of water-starved willows. The Weeping Willow, twice as tall, three times their breadth, dwarfed them.

Sturdy emerald leaves filled out the bountiful hanging limbs that hung in a heavy curtain. Everything the tree could reach, it touched: the creek bed, the parched red soil, the grass.

Birdie swung her light to scan what lay around the area. She inhaled sharply when she saw that any willow that dared encroach upon the Weeping Willow's territory was even more browned and feeble, as if the colossal tree siphoned the merest hint of water that graced this portion of Georgian land before any other plant life could be fed. Returning her attention to the tree, she found herself both fascinated and repulsed by its elegant malignance.

Marcel stepped forward. He steepled his fingers and drew in a breath, before addressing them.

"Witness, o tree of willow weeping,
We impassioned five seek our reaping.
Seer, singer, speaker, sculptor, server,
Bestow upon us the fruits of our fervor.
Willow, our body of work you inspire,
Imbue us with inspiration and fire."

In the ensuing silence, the wind whistled through the Weeping Willow's limbs and disturbed its stillness, brandishing its branches forward like outstretched fingers. Birdie's mouth grew dry. She swallowed over the lump in her throat.

"Did you come up with that yourself just now?" Dodge sashayed toward the makeshift campsite, singing. "*Witness, o tree of willow weeping.* Those would make killer song lyrics."

Adriana, Marcel, and Tom followed her. Birdie gazed up at the tree, her eyes tracing the dark outline against the night sky. The black, melded void of trunk and branches and leaves made her uneasy, yet she hesitated to wash the wan beam of her flashlight over it again. Tearing herself from her wary stare at the hulking form, she trudged after the group.

"Was it a poem?" Birdie asked.

Marcel held a hand to his stomach and bowed to her. "Indeed, my lady, it was. A poem and an intention." He brought his fingers to his lips, blowing a kiss to the stars.

Tom rolled his eyes as he gently set his cloaked sculpture down by the fire pit. The back of Birdie's neck still crept with a spooked, tickling sensation at the sight of it. It made her wish she'd never covered it back up with the cloth, blank limp body of wood that it was. Sometimes it was better to see the hideous details rather than be blind to them.

Dodge came up beside Tom. "We can gather some firewood and kindling."

"That would be great. I'll get the s'mores set up." Adriana set the picnic basket on the table. "Birdie, want to help me?"

"Sure." Birdie went over to Adriana, watching Tom and Dodge walk away. Her shoulders relaxed a little when she saw they weren't going too far, sticking to the outskirts of the clearing. She turned to Marcel. "What do you mean, *intention*?"

He positioned himself nearby in one of the collapsible camping chairs and crossed one leg over his knee. "What is life without intention? How will you know where to steer yourself?"

Adriana blew a puff of air up at a loose strand of hair that had come free from her ponytail. "*Ay, dios mío.* So grandiose all the time." She laid out the contents of the picnic basket on the table. Birdie spotted graham crackers, marshmallows, high-end chocolate bars filled with caramel, sea salt, fresh strawberries, and a jar of the Orchard Hill honey.

"Is there any other way to be?" Marcel stood and approached them, resting his hands on the table, his Cheshire grin and lighthearted wink aimed at Birdie. "Besides, you attract the energy you put out into the universe. We five have our undertaking laid before us. Why not tap into the creative spirits surrounding us to assist us to our end?"

Birdie bit her lip. She knew his words had been harmless; all the same, when he'd said them, she could have sworn the air took on an altered quality. As if the pressure changed, the breeze gathered strength, and the atmosphere shifted imperceptibly. She rubbed away the goose bumps on her arms, amazed she could shiver in the summer heat.

"Birdie?" Adriana peered at her. Only then did Birdie notice the plates and napkins being offered to her. "Could you arrange these and then help me put the ingredients in a row of bowls? It'll help make it like a station so each person can build their unique s'more."

As Birdie did so, Marcel settled back into his chair, his hands laced together behind his head and his eyes closed. Dodge and Tom returned, Dodge with an armful of twigs and broken branches for kindling and Tom with several thicker branches for firewood.

Tom kneeled by the fire pit and positioned their collection. He grabbed a bottle of lighter fluid and doused the kindling before lighting a match and throwing it on the pile. Birdie squinted as the flames flared, then settled. The fire took hold and cast up a billow of smoke into the sky, followed by the stray sparkling embers that floated into the air and sizzled out.

Warm light glowed upon the faces of her newfound group. Whether they'd become friends remained to be seen. Birdie had come with the intention of doing her work quietly and quickly, getting the leg up on her creative career she so desperately needed and then leaving. It was an invaluable opportunity. To ensure she made the most of every bit of it, she planned to be head down, nose to the grindstone. What use did she have for these people to be her friends?

Yet, despite her desire to keep her distance, the budding warmth of the fire reflected in her chest. Marcel was dramatic, but she found something so freeing in that. He'd seen her. Tom, grumpy as he was, felt kindred. He understood rural Georgia, the land, the soul, in a way none of the others grasped. Adriana put love into her food, and it showed. She possessed talent and a confident intellect in an unapologetic way that Birdie admired.

Birdie finished setting up the table. Dodge, now sitting in a chair between Tom and Marcel, said something that made Marcel laugh and even put a smirk on Tom's face. Dodge, off-putting and boundary pushing, made Birdie curious. Every time she thought she knew the type of woman Dodge was, Dodge did something unexpected. Perhaps this residency would be just what she needed. A breakthrough for her photography and a chance to live a little.

"Adriana," Birdie said, picking up the tiny jar of honey. "What kind of dessert do you think you'll make with this in your restaurant?"

Her hip cocked to the side, Adriana rested her

hand on it while tapping the other to her lips. "I've got a couple of ideas brewing that I'd like to test out while I'm here. You really liked it, did you?"

"Oh, yes," Birdie said.

Adriana's smiled broadened. *"Bueno, bueno."* A conspiratorial look came over her face, and she held one hand up to the side of her mouth. "You want to know a secret? They say this honey is very special. It allows you to see the dead."

Birdie shifted her weight, raising her brow. "Really?"

"No, not really. But it's going to make a great attraction for my restaurant. Customers will eat that up." Adriana's shoulders shook with laughter. "Literally!"

Before Birdie could respond, movement out of the corner of her eye caught her attention. A reverent Tom cradled his sculpture in both arms. She didn't have time to process what was happening until he tossed it into the fire. Flames shot high into the air, consuming the artwork. The cloth melted away like a dripping candle to reveal the charring woven creature in inanimate terror as its wooden flesh burned.

Heat blasted Birdie's face. Her skin grew fever hot and tight. The white scorching light seared her eyes, and she clasped her hands over them in agony.

5

"Birdie! Birdie, are you okay?" Arms encircled her shoulders. Eased to sit on the ground by someone she could not see, Birdie cradled her face in her hands. Her eyes stung, and tears streamed down her cheeks. Distantly, she thought perhaps it was Dodge's voice that reacted first.

"What happened?" Marcel asked.

"I don't know." Adriana, her accent heavier when she sounded worried, continued. "We were just finishing up the s'mores station."

"The fire." Birdie's voice came out in a croak.

"Here, let me get you some water," Adriana said.

"Tom, did you have to throw your sculpture in like some ridiculous funeral pyre?" The arms that held Birdie tightened. It was Dodge. Birdie stiffened, then leaned into the woman.

"What do you think I carried it all the way out here for?" Tom stomped closer in his thumping boots. Then his voice softened. "Is she burned? She wasn't that close to the fire."

Dodge touched Birdie's hand. "You aren't burned, are you? Can you try showing me?"

Birdie pressed her hands against her eyelids, her

cheeks, a moment longer. Whereas she would've sworn she was badly burned from the flare, now her skin felt unharmed, if only a little sweaty from holding her face. Slowly, she let Dodge pull down her hands while she kept her eyes closed. Dodge placed a water bottle in her palm, and Birdie drank from it hungrily.

Gentle fingers inspected her forehead, her temple, the tender flesh of her eyelids. "You're a little pink, but it doesn't seem like you're blistering or anything like that. Do you want to try opening your eyes?"

Birdie's stomach flopped. She couldn't keep her eyes closed forever, nor would she want to. But opening them and finding that she was somehow blinded—her heart sped like she was teetering on a cliff's edge.

Gripping Dodge's forearm, Birdie opened her eyes.

Like a sunburst, the campfire came into view, and she squinted. Dodge stayed steady at her side. Then Birdie blinked a couple of times, and Dodge's face came into focus, her eyes narrowed in concern, her chestnut hair wild. Marcel, Adriana, and Tom hovered nearby. With a tight breath still caught in her throat, Birdie exhaled bit by bit as she detected no abnormalities in her vision.

As she started to get up, Dodge helped her stand. "I think I'm okay. I'm sorry about that, you all. My eyes can be sensitive sometimes, I guess."

Adriana swooped over to the table and grabbed a plate. "Here, Tom will cook up a marshmallow for your s'more. Eat some chocolate. It'll make you feel better."

Birdie nibbled on a piece of dark chocolate as

Tom and Marcel skewered marshmallows and toasted them over the fire. Dodge nudged Birdie's shoulder and filled her plate with strawberries and caramels. "You sure you're okay, love? This place is really shaking you up, huh?"

Rubbing at her eyes, Birdie frowned. She had panicked earlier in the house and now this. A hot blush blossomed on her cheeks. "I—"

Dodge touched her arm. "It's okay." She glanced over her shoulder at the other three, then up at the Weeping Willow. "It's a lot to take in. A big change for all of us. Eat your sugar and get some rest tonight. It'll look different in the light of day."

"Thank you," Birdie whispered, but Dodge was already joining the others by the campfire to prepare her own marshmallow. Birdie turned her back to the fire while she ate a graham cracker. The blaze cast sharp edges on the Weeping Willow's leaves, changing the feathery boa branches into fiery wind chimes.

A breeze sighed through the leaves, and Birdie caught a glimpse of brass near the base of the tree. Puzzled, she strayed from her post by the s'mores station and moved closer to inspect it. Pulling out her flashlight, she saw that someone had screwed a bronze plate, no bigger than a business card, to the trunk. Roots encroached upon the tarnished metal, nearly swallowing the words. Birdie cleared them back, finding it much harder than she expected, as if the tree resisted her efforts. She mouthed the cursive words engraved into the plaque as she read them.

"Take from the Weeping Willow, and the Weeping Willow will take from you."

Her heart skipped a beat, and she blinked several times to make sure she'd read the inscription correctly. She stuttered, her first instinct to call everyone over, then clamped her mouth shut. Birdie looked to the fire, she herself shrouded in the tree's shadow, and watched the four artists eating and enjoying themselves. Was she really going to cause an alarm a third time in one day, the very first day of them meeting, the first day of their residency? She envisioned the next three months together, them never letting her forget what a nervous nelly she'd been. It'd be miserable.

Opening and closing her hands several times, she wished away the numbness and tingling crawling up her fingertips, a warning sign that her stress levels were too high. Birdie inhaled and exhaled deeply a few times. Perhaps the meaning behind the words wasn't intended to be as foreboding as they were in the depths of the night. It could be the work of an overzealous preservationist. Or some local trying to scare trespassers off. She'd look at it one more time and then put it behind her. It wasn't a big deal.

Yet, when Birdie cast her light back onto the tree base, her breath came in quick gasps. The bronze plate was gone. It was as if it never existed. Bulging roots, intertwined and knotted, sat in its place. The edges of her vision blurred, and she knew she had to calm her breathing or else she was going to pass out.

It couldn't be happening now. Not this soon. She had her whole photography career ahead of her. The foundation of her future, her potential, shifted as if built on grains of sand. She needed more time. If she couldn't trust her own eyes, how could she capture the beauty of the world around her?

Birdie rubbed her eyelids. Then she straightened and gritted her teeth. Maybe she'd imagined it. It had been a very long day, she hadn't eaten much —even then, it was all sugar—and heat could do things to a person, especially if one was already running on fumes.

Even if these were early symptoms, she resolved to do all she could in three months and create her best photographic series to date. After that... Her stomach fluttered, and bile rose in her throat... After would be just that: after.

Marcel called to her and waved her over. "It's time for a ghost story, my lovelies. Gather 'round."

Each of them congregated around the fire pit, settling into the folding chairs, Tom still eating his s'more and Adriana sharing a plate of strawberries with Dodge.

When Birdie arrived at the last empty chair, Marcel stood at the helm and wiggled his eyebrows. "Are you ready to hear about our mysterious benefactress? Tonight I'm going to regale you with the tale of the disappearance of Willa Cromwell."

6

The wind picked up, and the temperature dropped enough that Birdie surprised herself by wishing for a cardigan to cover the gooseflesh on her arms. Reluctantly she drew her chair close to the fire by Dodge, who welcomed her by rubbing her hands together and nodding in sympathy.

Marcel paced in a semicircle around the fire pit, his jacquard vest glimmering in the yellow light, turning the finely woven threads into molten gold. "Seer. Singer. Server. Sculptor." He tipped his head to each of them in kind, before performing an elegant cross between a curtsy and a bow, one arm held across his stomach and one against his back. "Speaker."

Out of the corner of her eye, Birdie saw Tom roll his eyes again. She might've joined him or Dodge in her approving smirk, yet when Marcel spoke, he emanated conviction and charm, commanding the audience to listen with rapt attention. Part of her felt she would've liked to listen to him discuss any topic. Another part held a deep foreboding within, as if they shouldn't air the dirty laundry of the person who afforded them this opportunity. Her feelings were rooted in more than just bad taste. Birdie was having a visceral reaction to what Marcel was about to say.

"I relay to you now, in a far more eloquent fashion mind you, the story shared with me in town. We've all gleaned that Ms. Willa Cromwell was an eccentric woman. In her will, or so we've been told, she left instructions to be followed to the exact letter for a grant. A three-month artists residency would be held fifty years after her will was executed, the fiftieth anniversary of her death. Why fifty? No one I've spoken to has given me anything resembling a satisfying answer."

Birdie meekly raised her hand, casting a quick glance back at the Weeping Willow. "Marcel, I don't mean to interrupt, but are you sure we should be talking about this? It doesn't seem right to talk about the dead."

"Ah." Marcel raised a finger in the air. "But *is* she dead? I get ahead of myself."

Dodge jabbed Birdie in the rib lightly and offered an impish grin. "Relax. It's okay to live a little."

Birdie frowned and turned to Adriana for support, but she was too busy paying attention to Marcel. Tom only shrugged at Birdie's wordless plea.

Marcel splayed the fingers on his right hand and hopped up on a nearby tree stump. "Five! Five artists of different disciplines must congregate and create masterpieces in their varying mediums inspired by the willow trees surrounding Willow Creek Mansion. And that, my darlings, is what summoned us here together tonight, as well as where our knowledge of the strange woman who is offering an opportunity for our art to bloom ends." He lowered his chin and narrowed his eyes, pitching shadows underneath his brow and giving him a devilish glare. "Until now."

Birdie wiped her sweaty hands on her jeans and pretended to be cool. She pictured crawling into bed after the evening festivities were over, falling into a dreamless sleep, and waking early the next morning to spend time on the grounds alone, with only her camera by her side. She focused on easing the tension in her muscles despite a strong inclination to resist.

"The final branch in a lush family tree of accomplished and enchanting artists, Willa lacked these creative qualities to such a severe degree that her paternity in the Cromwell bloodline was questioned. Though no other fatherly suspects ever seemed justified, as Willa's mother spent vast amounts of time with her beloved willow trees when she wasn't otherwise occupied with the upkeep of running Willow Creek Mansion. Hence the name Willa.

"Compared to her striking mother, Willa's face was plain and forgettable. Her hair is said to have been duller than the dullest brown of a tree trunk; her gaze so flat and lacking spark that those in town avoided it at all costs. Next to her father, she was a veritable void of talent. No artwork she ever attempted amounted to anything worthy of awe in his eyes.

"After Willa, her mother never again conceived, despite every effort to the contrary. When her parents passed, they had no choice but to leave Willow Creek Mansion, the family lands, and their legacy to a daughter, who by all accounts and evidence, was destined to sap the family name of all its splendor."

Marcel jumped down from the stump and

stalked like a cat in front of his audience. "Except! Willa had one extraordinary quality which no one could deny her." Marcel stared into the fire, and Birdie watched the flames reflect in his eyes. Still uneasy, she couldn't help but recognize that Marcel was in his element—*this* was his art. "*Passion,*" he said. "Passion ignited within her with such ferocity that all others paled in comparison. No longer restrained by her parents, Willa hired every artist of every kind within a hundred miles."

Continuing on a loop around the campfire, Marcel paused behind Birdie and rested his hands on her shoulders. She longed to turn around or shrug him off, but instead sat very still. "The process and request were the same for each. Willa would guide them as they created her portrait. It's said she would hover..." Marcel bent down near Birdie's ear. "And whisper to them every paint stroke, every placement, every angle and color used."

When Marcel stood and followed along the ring of chairs until he came back to his original spot, Birdie hid a shudder. The idea of someone taking that much control over her art, suffocating and warping what she captured through the lens, would smother any joy from the experience. As she looked at the others, she saw much of the same revulsion reflected on their faces.

With a swooping motion, Marcel gestured toward the path that led back to the mansion. "You can see many of those portraits on display in the foyer today. According to the townsfolk, not one of these artists satisfied Willa with their depiction of her likeness. With each iteration, she grew more frenzied, more stern, encouraging the artists to push all boundaries of art. None of them came close to her vision, and lacking the talent to make it come to life herself, Willa's grip on her sanity unraveled. Rumors emerged that she'd moved beyond the limits of art into darker realms of creativity."

A branch in the waning fire snapped, and Adriana yipped. Tom jumped. When they realized what had happened, Dodge laughed, followed by Marcel and the others, a nervous release of tension. Birdie, proud of herself that she didn't startle, joined in. Yet the laughter sounded inauthentic in her ears. She closed her eyes against a flashing vision, back to the haunting portrait on the wall. Even if the story Marcel was telling was true, there's no way Willa had been that far gone.

Marcel held a finger to his lips until they simmered down. "As you can imagine, several of these artists shared their increasingly disturbing experiences with those in town. If there are any two qualities you can rely on in a human being, they are our ability to gripe and to gossip.

"Word spread faster than the roots of a tree, entangling the townsfolk in Ms. Cromwell's affairs. Then, the time frame that the artists spent at Willow Creek Mansion grew longer and longer. Whispers filled the streets, and wonders ran rampant. '*When was the last one seen? Hasn't it been more than a week?*'" Marcel held his hand up to the side of his mouth, calling out these questions to the left and the right.

A fox screamed in the distance. Birdie bit her lip. She didn't want to hear the rest. Adriana pressed a hand to her heart. "My dear Marcel, you do remember that we have to sleep in this place."

He waved his hand at her dismissively. "I'm almost done." He smoothed the front of his vest. "One day, an artist that had been gone so long, they'd nearly forgotten she was out there at Willow Creek Mansion, wandered into town. She limped down the road, a shoe missing, her shirt torn, her face dirty, and hair tousled wild. Mumbling to herself, the townsfolk wouldn't have believed her if it weren't for all the other accounts.

"This woman, having displeased Willa with her portrait, was locked in a cramped wooden box in complete darkness by the creek." Marcel hunched down and contorted himself as small as possible. "Willa held her there against her will, in complete sensory deprivation, and was told she'd have to stay there until she fully comprehended how precious her creative talents were.

"No light, no sound, no feeling, no eating." Marcel ticked his fingers as he emphasized each. "This wasn't the first victim of Willa's brutal passion. She was simply the first to have been held so long, she bordered on a breakdown. That night, fueled by the frightening tales of her sensory deprivation box, the townsfolk descended upon Willow Creek Mansion. Under a full moon, they dragged Ms. Cromwell down to the creek, perhaps even right over here..."

Marcel stooped and grazed the dirt with his fingertips. He clapped, the sound echoing in the trees. "They locked her up in her own box in the dead of night and left her there. Their reasoning: give her a dose of her own medicine so she'd never do that to anyone else again. However, their plan backfired."

Shadows stretched around the fire pit as the fire died down further. Birdie wrapped her arms around herself. She squinted to make out Marcel's features by the light of the simmering logs.

"When they returned that morning to release her from the prison of her own creation, the box was empty. No one could figure out how she'd escaped. Did she have a secret key? Did someone come for her? They entered the mansion, calling her name, searching for the deranged woman." Marcel grew somber, lowering his voice. "Yet the only sign of Willa Cromwell was her blood splattered will, the very will detailing the instructions of our grant and residency. No one ever saw her again."

Marcel paused and made eye contact with each one of them. "Was she murdered? Split town? Speculation among the locals is still hotly debated. Some even suggest something *much darker* happened." He brushed his hands together, signifying the conclusion of his tale. "Either way, the legacy of Ms. Willa Cromwell's passion now squarely rests in our hands. We have a chance to show her how passion and art can truly come together to make something extraordinary."

Adriana rose from her chair and flicked on her flashlight. "Sí. Without involving torture."

Marcel chuckled, and he and Tom started to help Adriana pack up. "Yes. But it makes for a titillating tale, does it not?"

Dodge slapped her knee. "Heck yeah, it does. That's some great stuff there, Marcel. Definitely gets those artistic juices flowing. Don't you think, Birdie?"

"Hmm?" She stared over at the Weeping Willow, thinking she'd heard something and chalking it up to the wind rustling through the leaves. However, the air was thick and stifling. "That box, the darkness. It must've been horrible."

Adriana clucked her tongue. "It's not real, sweetie. Right, Marcel?"

He shrugged, sprightly laughter twinkling in his eyes. "Who knows?"

Tom grumbled, looping Adriana's picnic basket over his large forearm. "We can leave the lighter and lighter fluid out here for next time. It'll be fine under the table." He led them back to the path. "It's disappointing. Can you really even call that a ghost story, Marcel? There's no ghost."

Marcel sighed in dramatic fashion, somehow managing to be both condescending and sweet. "My darling, hasn't anyone told you? Not all ghost stories need to be about literal ghosts."

7

Before Birdie opened her eyes to the sun's warmth prodding through her window, she heard the *squeak, clank, hiss* of the shower turning on in the adjoining bathroom. Pipes rumbled under the strain of being asked to perform after a long period of disuse. Not long after, Dodge hummed a melody, adding a verse here or there. Birdie felt strange hearing a work in progress. Birdie's own work involved capturing what existed. Whether she played with angles or light, she only sought to show what was and only shared when she was ready. The art of a musician evolved as it was created—the artist had to possess such vulnerability and openness to share something not perfected, not final.

Birdie was undecided on whether being an unwilling audience to Dodge's process annoyed her. Then a stray lyric failed to land a rhyme and Birdie winced. She sighed and stretched, enjoying the feeling of the stark white plush comforter and sheets on the queen-size bed. They reminded her of hotel linens, and perhaps she wasn't so far off. Anything not distinctly identifiable as part of the original fixtures appeared to have been brand new and commercially made. Those items were few and far between, however.

Her suitcase sat in the corner, and she ignored her inclination to unpack further, settle in, and ready herself for the day. She'd meant to be up early and sneak out to capture the sunrise and surroundings. Rolling over, she snuggled the blankets and faced the window. Too late for that, based on the brightness of the sun outside. Maybe if she slept in, she could slip out later without having to interact with anyone. Marcel's story lingered to the point where just when she'd put it out of her mind, the eeriness of it all circled back around to disturb her.

The long, gauzy curtains floated in the light breeze from the window, ghostly companions in the daylight. With her door closed, she'd been forced to open the sill or sweat through her pajamas. It'd also let the sounds of the night follow her to bed, including the screaming foxes. Sleep threatened an encore as she watched the curtains dance. The shadows of branches fell upon the cream fabric like crooked, waving fingers.

Dodge shrieked, and Birdie's drooping eyelids flew open.

Throwing aside the covers, she hopped up, bare feet slapping on the warped wood, and went to the bathroom door. "Are you okay? Can I come in?" Her hand was already on the brass knob.

Breathless, Dodge answered. "Yes."

Birdie entered and scanned the bathroom. It was rather large, she'd daresay rivaling the size of their rooms. A hulking claw-foot porcelain tub was planted in the center, directly in front of the floor-to-ceiling windows. The tub had a shower curtain and a shower head that dropped down from the center of the ceiling. Deep double sinks punctuated the wall-to-wall vanity opposite the windows. A waist-high privacy wall blocked off the toilet. This is where Birdie found Dodge.

Dodge stared at the toilet, clasping her towel around her, her wet curls dripping on the floor. Birdie didn't see any blood or cause for alarm. Yet Dodge didn't take her eyes off the toilet as Birdie approached.

Touching her shoulder lightly, Birdie spoke to Dodge. "Hey, what's wrong? I heard you scream."

Dodge jumped at her touch, then calmed. "I thought I saw something. I could've sworn it was...a tree root?"

Birdie looked from the empty toilet bowl to Dodge, heat rimming her ears and blotching on her cheeks. Her hands became numb. "Oh," was all she managed before turning heel and heading back to her room.

Footfalls followed her, and Birdie wished she'd shut the door behind her. "Where are you going?"

Busying herself in her suitcase, Birdie lay out her clothes for the day. Dodge stood between her and the bed. "Excuse me," Birdie said, ducking around Dodge and heading for her camera equipment.

"But what about what I saw?" Dodge asked.

Birdie stopped and gave Dodge a heated glare. "What about what you saw? I know what this is. You're making fun of me. And I don't appreciate it."

A softness emerged in Dodge's expression that only made Birdie not want to face her all the more. "*Birdie*. That's not what I'm doing. I really did see something...or I thought I did." Dodge sat on the edge of the bed. Why wasn't she leaving? The conversation was clearly over. "So did you sleep okay?"

"Sure." Birdie mumbled, throwing in a heavy dash of sarcasm, and picked up her camera.

Dodge continued as if Birdie were being more engaging than she was. "Yeah, I couldn't sleep either. Darn foxes howling like banshees." She lifted a finger in the air, and her eyes lit up. "Ooh! That's a good lyric. I'll have to write that down."

Birdie watched Dodge sprint to her room and return with a pen and paper. While she jotted down her notes, Birdie frowned. "Do you have siblings?"

"What?" Dodge glanced up. "Oh yes, three sisters!"

"That's what I thought." Birdie grabbed her toothbrush and headed into the bathroom.

"Why? Do you have any?" Dodge called to her.

She paused in her brushing. "No."

Birdie heard Dodge chuckle. "And that's what *I* thought." She appeared around the doorjamb behind Birdie, who looked at her in the mirror's reflection. "You definitely have the aura of an only child about you."

"An aura?" Birdie asked.

Dodge traced her hands around Birdie in an outline. "It's not a bad thing. Just different. I sense a high level of independence. A little lonesome. Very intuitive." Crossing through the bathroom, Dodge continued to talk while getting dressed. Birdie caught movement of clothing but looked away to give the woman her privacy. "You should let me read your cards."

"What do you mean? Like tarot?" Birdie had flirted with going to a psychic once in Atlanta but had decided against it at the last minute. It seemed silly, and she couldn't justify the expenditure.

Entering the bathroom in jeans and a plaid button-down, Dodge hopped up to sit on the counter. "Kind of like tarot. I prefer to use oracle decks. You'll love it." She touched her chest. "It breaks through all the noise of the day and gets to the real heart of things."

Birdie raised an eyebrow. Dodge was so sincere, she had to smile. "Okay. If you say so."

"I do." Dodge clapped her hands and rubbed them together. "Any idea what direction your photography project might take?"

She leaned against the counter and considered the question. "Not really. There's a lot of great flora and fauna on the grounds I want to explore. Tying it to the willow trees will be interesting." A chill flitted down Birdie's spine. She had an eagerness to take pictures of anything but the trees: cicadas, dried red creek beds, and the old shed. She'd take every inch of them over the willows.

Dodge kicked her feet playfully against the counter. "Have you ever done any ghost photography?"

Birdie rolled her eyes. "No. There are just some things you don't mess with. Most of it is baloney anyway. Deceit in service of sensationalism." She gathered her toiletries and headed back to her room. "Besides, isn't there enough wonder in the world without playing tricks on your eyes?"

8

Birdie avoided eye contact with the judgmental stare of several dozen Willa Cromwell portraits as she hurried down the staircase and into the foyer. She held her camera to keep it from bouncing against her chest. Though her stomach growled at the smells of freshly baked pastries and coffee wafting from the kitchen, she tiptoed to the door in an attempt to slink out before encountering any other of the mansion's tenants. All she wanted to hear was the steady trickle of the low creek waters and the buzzing of summer insects in the air.

Quiet talking coming from the hall leading to the kitchen reached her ears, and she didn't think they'd noticed her. She turned the knob carefully, but when she opened the door, it creaked with such ferocity that she may as well have rung the doorbell.

"Birdie?" Adriana popped her head around the corner. She beckoned her over. "Come, come. I've made peach turnovers, and coffee is brewing."

Birdie hesitated, then closed the door. She did plan to be out for quite a while, and maybe it couldn't hurt to bolster her reserves with a stiff coffee. Walking into the kitchen, she spotted Marcel hunched at the table, a stylish turquoise cowl hanging over his head. "Your turnovers smell heavenly, Adriana."

"Don't they though?" Adriana handed Birdie a plate with two pastries, as well as a mug of steaming coffee. "Cream and sugar are on the table."

"Thanks." Birdie smiled. She slid into a chair across from Marcel who hadn't looked up at or addressed her since she'd entered. For the first time, she noticed he was hovering over a bowl and inhaling. She took a sip of her coffee, savoring it. When he still didn't look up, she frowned. The quiet felt too large; she'd already grown used to him filling it with his eloquent words. "Marcel? You okay?"

He breathed in again deeply, and Birdie realized steam emanated from the bowl. Adriana, cleaning dishes in the sink, spoke up. "Marcel's not feeling too hot this morning. I boiled some water for him to see if it helps his throat."

Marcel lifted his head, his sorrow-filled eyes landing on Birdie. When he talked, his voice held nowhere near the force and charisma she'd witnessed last night. Instead it was cracked and shaky. He ran his fingers along his throat. "My allergies must be acting up. Or I'm coming down with a cold."

Dodge sailed into the kitchen, snagged a turnover from the counter, and patted Marcel on the back. "Maybe it's because you talked too much last night, buddy."

Marcel fake-laughed at her and pursed his lips. "Just you stay away, honey. If it's a cold, you don't want to get it. What's a folk singer without her voice?"

Dodge scooted her chair dramatically away from

him and nodded. "You ain't wrong." She bit into her turnover. "So good, chef. Thank you kindly."

Adriana nodded to her. "Happy to."

"Where's Tom on this fine morning?" Dodge asked.

"He's out working on his new sculpture already. He seems to get going before sunrise." Adriana handed Birdie a thermos. "You're eager to get out there too; I can tell. Thought you might want a to-go cup." She winked at Birdie.

Birdie's heart warmed at the thoughtfulness. "Thank you." She stood, pushed her chair in, and took her dishes to the counter. Dodge chatted with or rather to Marcel as she left. "I'll be gone for a couple hours. Let me know if I can help with lunch or dinner later?"

Drying her hands on a towel slung over her shoulder, Adriana smiled. "That would be lovely." She patted a time-worn book on the counter. Its edges were tattered, and loose-leaf pages hung askew. "I found this old cookbook in the kitchen drawers. I was thinking about trying out a dessert recipe from it if you're willing to go on a little cooking adventure with me. It calls for some really interesting local ingredients I've never used before."

"Sure. That could be fun," Birdie said, surprised that she meant it. She took up her thermos. When she passed the tray of turnovers, she paused and backed up to help herself to one more. Adriana left her with another wink, and Birdie exited the mansion in unexpectedly high spirits. Today was going to be a good day. She just knew it.

9

The sun dazzled the front lawn in brilliant tans, umbers, and burnt siennas. Tall, stiff grasses swayed as the heat of the day settled over the grounds of Willow Creek like a weighted blanket. Birdie tread through them, enjoying the soft crunch they made as she stepped onto infrequently trodden portions of the yard. Their sand-colored blades parted to reveal the red Georgian clay underneath, shattered with cracks like a broken mirror.

She crouched and lifted her camera's lens, then snapped a few photos of the effect. Up close, she mused that it was like collecting photos of the broken capillaries of the southern land, so parched for water that it had split itself wide open to drink up every drop of liquid that should grace its surface. When Birdie rose, she spun slowly and pondered which direction she might like to wander toward next.

Her feet carried her around the side of the mansion, along the path they'd followed last night to the campsite. As she entered the backyard—which was a severe understatement of what was essentially a wild, sprawling field behind the mansion bordered by the path, woods, and creek—the sunlight cast off the adumbral cloak from the exterior and draped the deteriorating building in tawny organic tapestry.

Birdie watched her step as she worked her way to stand in the middle and appreciate the fierceness with which nature sought to reclaim the land. Like great sea serpents, willow tree roots reared themselves through the red clay as they traveled across the yard and toward the foundation of the mansion. She kneeled and ran her hand along the back of one of the roots. It was much wider than any other she'd ever seen. A thick mat of offshoot filaments spread around it, whitish and oddly ticklish to the touch.

She followed the root system. Where the earth opened in clay cracks, she found more mats of roots. Even if someone wanted to clear out and tidy the lawn, it would be near impossible to mow; the roots would almost surely clog any mower that attempted the job. When she examined the slats on the back of the house, Birdie saw that the roots had worked themselves in between the siding, causing it to loosen and sag. It would take a ton of effort to repair the damage. She wondered what the mansion looked like in its prime, before nature began eating away at its edges.

After snapping several photos, which she didn't hate but didn't think were the direction she was going to go in for her project, she faced away from Willow Creek Mansion and sipped her coffee from the thermos. The path and creek ran along her left. Ahead, the shed marred the landscape, its remnants keeping her from imagining the time and place without the touch of humans. She cocked her head to the side and considered that the contents could provide interesting photographic subjects, however.

As she approached the shed, she noticed it was once painted red, evident by the scant flakes of paint on the wood. The lean wasn't as bad as she previously thought. The shed had two grimy windows on each side and a door with a fat, rusting padlock. Birdie tugged on the lock to no avail. Biting her lip, she went to one of the windows and wiped the dirt off one of the four square panes. Through the clouded glass, she only got a hazy picture of its contents: a couple of old axes piled against the wall, stacked papers, cans and cans of what must've been paint, brushes, and all sorts of other tools which could've either been for yard work or creative work. It was difficult to tell.

Birdie tried the window and found it wouldn't budge; it was either locked or simply wedged shut from time and weather damage. The same was true of the other window. Guessing it was time to move on, the sun now high in the sky and sweat beading on her skin, she shuffled through the dense grasses along the side of the shed, thinking to head toward the path. The toe of her boot caught on something that produced a metallic jingle.

Bending over, Birdie discovered the tinkling came from a large ring cluttered with quite a few old keys. Puzzled, she looked around as if she'd find any clue as to why they'd be out here. She held them up and brushed some red dirt from their handles. The filagree on them was intricately interwoven, and she thought perhaps the curved semicircle inlaid within might be a *C* for Cromwell. As she slipped the keys into a front pouch on her camera bag, she startled.

A shadow crossed the opposite shed window.

It'd only been a quick movement, caught in the corner of her eye. Hand to heart, she breathed and tried to calm herself. It could've been anything; she'd seen it through murky glass, through a dark shed. Maybe it was a cloud? Birdie cast her eyes to the pale blue, cloudless sky. Her hands grew clammy, nothing of which had to do with the increasing humidity of the day.

She tiptoed around the back of the shed, moving as silently as she could manage in the starched grasses, and peeked around the other side. Her shoulders slumped, and she let out the breath she'd been holding.

Nothing was there.

Still, she scanned around for any signs of what could've caused the shadow. She adjusted the camera strap around her neck and fiddled with the zipper on the pouch she'd just put the key ring in. She'd been preoccupied with the keys and considered maybe she missed a hawk flying overhead.

Eager to leave the backyard and shed behind, the creeping sensation of movement out of her field of vision not dissipating no matter how many times she assured herself it was nothing, Birdie took to the trail and carried on toward the site of the campfire pit. The wilted, browning leaves of the willows along the path hadn't been as evident in the darkness of the evening prior. Now it was all she noticed.

How were they even still alive? She drifted from the path now and again to walk closer to the creek. The water was so low that she could almost walk along the bed itself. Here, the roots didn't appear strong, white, and searching like they did behind the mansion. Instead they crumbled to a powdery dust if she touched them, the poor things unable to complete the journey to reach the water that was only slightly above a dribble.

When her shoulders brushed their drab garlands of leaves, the willow trees abandoned them to the red clay. Sadness and desperation emitted from them such that Birdie returned to the trail and soon found herself drawn like a moth to the brazen emerald leaves of the Weeping Willow.

10

Birdie passed the charred fire pit, quiet and cold, a stark contrast to the blinding brilliance of last night's flames. The heat of midday found its stride, and the chairs and tables were hot to the touch. She meandered around the sticks they'd used to roast marshmallows, the lighter fluid, the tree stump that Marcel had given his speech from—delaying her inevitable approach to the willow.

Its weighty presence still heavy and strange in the light of day, the Weeping Willow had one appeal that was difficult for a southern girl to resist, despite its ability to send goose bumps across her arms. Unlike the other willows in the area, the Weeping Willow's dense leaves were strong enough to fend off the unforgiving August sun and provide a respite of shade from the grueling temperature.

She checked her watch and blinked. How could two and a half hours have passed since she'd left the house? Birdie tapped the glass surface, shook her head, and carried on to the trunk of the tree where she'd seen the sign embedded, then disappear. She'd been known to while away the hours when photographing subjects and materials that interested her, but this seemed excessive even for her.

Through the lens of her camera, Birdie eyed the willow and snapped a picture. Greens so deep they bordered on blue swayed against the backdrop of the clear sky. Framed by the soft browns surrounding it, the Weeping Willow almost bent toward her, it was so stark and stunning. She returned the camera to hang from the strap and rest on her chest, wondering at this odd phenomenon. How was it that this single tree overpowered all the rest in the quest for water during a dry season?

Her feet and lower back ached from walking too long, so she sat down and leaned against the Weeping Willow. Perhaps it would reveal to her its secrets on standing out above the rest surrounding it. The wind sighed around her, rustling the drooping garlands. Birdie sighed along with it and relaxed into the tree, which, to her unexpected relief, didn't resist. She laughed. Worrying about a tree not liking her and about spending too much time on her craft? Couldn't she just chill out and let herself enjoy something for once?

The pain in her soles eased, and she felt as if she'd found the perfect spot. The root formation cradled her, providing something close to arm rests, and conformed to her back. She observed the roots fanned outward from the tree. They dove underground about ten feet from the base of the trunk, spreading who knows how far from it. Birdie guessed they'd at least tapped into the creek nearby, no doubt playing a huge role in the willow flourishing in hard times.

She closed her eyes and rested her head against the bark. The air tasted rich with minerals from the red clay and smelled fresh from the willow's greenery, untouched by the pollution she'd grown accustomed to in the city. Her fingers wrapped around the roots at her sides. Something about the place spoke to her in a way that reached a part of her she'd long since given up on—*home.*

Birdie had always been rather transient since leaving the small southern Georgia town her parents raised her in. She'd flitted from city to city, reluctant to return to anywhere off the beaten path. Telling herself it was because a chance at a photography career was far more likely to take off in an urban location, she knew deep down that it was because she thought that quiet life made her uninteresting. No one had fostered her creativity then, or even shown a remote interest in it. No, it was far too impractical and flighty to create things for the sake of creating them. Better to spend her time contributing to the family so they could eat and be clothed, especially with her father's disability.

Dodge likely assumed Birdie wasn't great with sharing because she was a spoiled only child, but it was quite the opposite. Every shred of anything close to useful was to be hoarded, held away from the covetous eyes of others, precisely because of its rarity in her life.

She gripped the roots and felt their strength. The bronze-plated sign, which she was almost certain now she hadn't truly seen, had said, "Take from the Weeping Willow, and the Weeping Willow will take from you." What if she gave something instead—a secret always lingering on her lips but never voiced?

"I'm afraid I don't have what it takes to do this," she said aloud. A tear slid down her cheek. "But I'm more afraid that I won't even get to really try. I thought I had more time."

Once she said it, Birdie felt the stress and sadness flow out of her, through her hands, into the roots, into the Weeping Willow itself. It didn't take away the truth of it. Yet, anything was better than keeping her darkest fears bottled up a moment longer—even confessing them to a tree.

A cry from above sent her scrambling to her feet.

Her heart thumped against her ribcage. The sound hadn't been very far from her head. She swiveled up the camera to her eye, searching for the culprit.

Another cry. This time she identified it as the call of a bird—two long trills, followed by four low coos—and felt a little silly. Birdie unclenched her jaw and, curiosity piqued along with a desire to distract herself from her morose musings, kept an eye out for the bird. She started in closer to the trunk, checking in the nooks and crannies of the larger branches at shoulder height. At last, she spotted what she suspected might be nearby.

A nest.

Keeping her distance and using her camera lens to get a good look, she spied a bird the color of coffee with cream, speckled with black spots. She zoomed in. The bird bobbed its head and cooed some more, then rustled its feathers. Woven twigs, grass, and willow tree leaves formed the precarious nest, which sent Birdie's already agitated nerves further on edge.

She ducked as another bird, almost identical, swooped in over her head and landed on the row of tucked grasses forming the nest's ledge. After a brief exchange of coos, the sitting bird flew away. Her eyes widened at the sight of two small eggs, only the briefest of images before the other bird assumed its watch warming and protecting the precious contents. She hadn't realized there were birds in Georgia that laid eggs so late in the season. What miraculous luck.

Her mind whirled, struck by a sudden burst of creative inspiration. The eggs, and the hatchlings that surely must soon follow, would make an excellent collection of work. They'd made their home in the Weeping Willow, choosing the only tree bursting with life to begin new life.

It was *perfect*.

In a daze, she stepped back several paces. The wind picked up so quickly it stole her breath, then the gusts surged, forming a riotous fury that whipped her hair across her face and stung her cheeks. The leaves rattled until the sound merged in a loud, violent whisper. Her heel caught on a root, sending her tumbling backward. She shrieked. The bird in its nest cooed angrily, took flight, and dive-bombed her head.

Birdie threw her hands up to defend herself. Wings flapped, soft feathers and air battered her. She did her best to inch away and not hurt the poor, startled thing. Once the avian assault ceased, she lowered her arms and opened her eyes.

Pitch black.

She rubbed her eyes, waiting for the world to come into focus again.

Nothing.

She blinked repeatedly. Inky blackness closed in around her.

Birdie flung her arms out and was met with a solid wall within inches of her body. She jerked backward and slammed into another wall. Her adrenaline skyrocketed. She tried to stand and slammed her head into the ceiling. Her breath came in ragged gasps, and she clutched her chest. Despite the dark, small stars of light danced across her vision. If she didn't calm down, she was going to knock herself unconscious or faint.

Where was she? This was impossible. Her hand trembled as she reached out to touch the wall. As she ran her finger along it, she detected the rough grains of wood. Frantic, she explored every inch of her confinement. Wooden slats surrounded her on all sides.

Birdie was in a box. Willa's sensory deprivation box.

Cramped, crouched, and claustrophobic, Birdie screamed at the top of her lungs and squeezed her eyes shut.

She stayed like that for far too long. Her arms numbed from holding herself so tight. She told herself it wasn't real so many times that the words took on that funny quality any word does when repeated too much. Then, as the adrenaline slowly subsided, her mind registered the breeze again, gracing her skin. The air didn't feel enclosed; it felt open. Light pressed against her eyelids; she wasn't in complete darkness.

Birdie pried her eyes open, and the sun beamed down, painfully bright. She was right where she ought to have been before the nightmarish vision of the box. Even the root that had been the cause of her fall sat in front of her toes, mocking her. She spent a few minutes catching her breath and attempting to calm herself down. Her mind couldn't make sense of what had happened.

Licking her parched lips, Birdie checked her watch. Late afternoon? Her heart sped again. She tried to swallow and found it difficult with her mouth so dry. Brushing her hand across her forehead, she realized she wasn't sweating, despite the brutal heat. Confusion, dizziness… She'd lost track of time, and the only thing she'd had to drink all day was coffee.

Birdie would've smacked herself if she'd had the energy. She knew better than to let herself get to the point of heat exhaustion, but then she'd thought she'd only be a couple of hours, not all day. Silly that all those campfire tales got to her and made her interpret a fainting spell for something wicked and utterly ridiculous.

With a huge sigh, she got to her feet. When she was sure of her balance, she made her way back along the path to Willow Creek Mansion.

11

Birdie rushed up the porch steps, ignoring the soulful guitar melody and enchanting singing coming from the wicker bench nearby. The last thing she wanted to do was chat. She needed water. Sip, don't chug, she reminded herself, and knew she might not be able to hold back even though it was the smart move. She longed to go upstairs, rest, and look at the photos she'd taken during the day.

The song stopped as Birdie reached for the handle on the double doors. "Where you off to in such a scurry hurry?" Dodge asked.

Opening the door, Birdie glanced at Dodge, whose boots rested on the edge of the squat, weather-worn coffee table. "I need water..." Blood rushed to her head, and her knees, weak, began to give out beneath her. Darkness bled in the periphery of her field of vision till she could only see the faintest shape moving toward her.

Arms wrapped around her and guided her to a chair. The rim of a cool glass touched her lips, followed quickly by water. Birdie gulped it hungrily while Dodge released her to lean against the chair back. "Birdie, love, you've gotta start taking better care of yourself."

Birdie managed to slow herself; she'd regret downing the whole glass of water, even if it tasted like heaven. The last thing she wanted to do was throw up in front of Dodge. As Birdie set the glass on the table, Dodge settled back onto the bench, her guitar sitting upright next to her. Birdie wiped her mouth. "Thank you for the water. I just lost track of time while taking pictures. Didn't realize how the heat was getting to me."

Dodge nodded. "Can I see? There's some really cool stuff out here. I bet you got some excellent shots."

Birdie held her camera close. "Not now. I haven't even looked at them."

Holding up her hands in peace, Dodge smirked. "I get it. Most artists don't like to share their works-in-progress."

"Well..." Birdie turned on her camera and flicked to the one picture she knew was dazzling no matter who you were. She didn't want Dodge to think of her as this spoiled only child, unable to share at all. Add to that overly sensitive and a little weird, and Birdie cringed inside. Maybe it was true; those were facets of her personality. But they weren't everything. She could be fun; she could be personable. "Maybe I can give you a peek at one."

Birdie flipped the screen around so Dodge could see and showed her the image of the Weeping Willow, its leaves shimmering like carved jade against the baby blue sky. When Birdie heard Dodge's intake of breath—awe that came from a real place, not overly exaggerated platitudes—Birdie smiled.

"You like it?" Birdie asked.

Dodge put her hand on Birdie's arm. "Like it?" Her eyes brimmed with excitement. "I *love* it. It's amazing, Birdie."

"Thanks." Birdie tucked away her camera in her bag. When she looked up, she noticed Dodge staring at her but couldn't quite discern the meaning behind the expression on her face. It was almost concern, yet there was a dash of pity and lingering excitement like she wanted to say something but was holding back. "What's up?" Birdie frowned.

Dodge laughed. "Am I so obvious?" She bent forward and grabbed a deck of cards off the table that Birdie hadn't noticed. "I have an idea brewing. I'm not ready to share it yet though. First..." Dodge shuffled the embossed cards, the gilded edges glittering. The backs were midnight blue and littered with gold stars and crescent moons. "Can I do your reading now? You look like you could use it."

"I look like I could use it?" Birdie furrowed her brow. An unusual urge to defend herself instead of simply retreat flared inside her chest. "Dodge, has anyone ever told you that you're good at pressing people's buttons?"

Dodge's mouth clamped shut, and her eyes went wide. Then she pursed her lips, which devolved into her usual wry grin. "Damn, girl." She laughed, and Birdie couldn't help but smile too. "I like this zesty side of you. You should let her out more."

"Ha, I wish." Birdie rolled her eyes and took a sip of water. "Okay, so what do I do?"

Dodge placed her fingers on the top of the deck and held them out to Birdie. "Put your hand on mine and ask a question."

"Ask a question? Like what?"

"Hmmm..." Dodge tapped the cards with the tip

of her fingernail. "How about something about your photography? These cards are really good when it comes to creative endeavors."

Birdie paused, then nodded. "Where will my photography career take me?" As soon as she said it, she chuckled nervously and withdrew her hand. She felt silly.

Yet Dodge's face fell serious. She shuffled the cards a few more times, fanned the deck out wide, and took her time choosing three cards, hovering over them, and then darting in like they spoke to her. Birdie held her breath. She wiped her hands on her jeans, then stopped, self-conscious, aware it was a nervous tic of hers.

Her hand poised over the first card she'd pulled, Dodge flipped it over. The whimsical illustration depicted a fair maiden with long golden hair down her back, standing next to a flowing river in a mystical forest, her arm outstretched to a white dove in mid-flight. At the top, in inked calligraphy, was the card's title. "Nature's bond," Dodge announced. "Good card. This means that you'll have strong ties with the natural life around you: plants, animals, the earth, the air."

Birdie studied the card. "That's kind of cool. I was actually thinking I'd focus on a pair of birds I'd found nesting in a willow tree." She left out that it was the Weeping Willow, unsure what Dodge would think of it.

"The cards do have a way of connecting more than we expect from random chance. That's why I like pulling them. They show us what we need to know." Dodge moved to the second card. "Ready?"

Birdie nodded.

Dodge turned over the next card.

Birdie stood so fast her chair tipped over, clattering hollowly on the porch floorboards. Her blood ran cold and the dizziness from earlier returned. "I can't do this."

She started for the front door, but Dodge caught her arm. "What's wrong?"

The sincere concern on Dodge's face calmed Birdie. "I—" She forced herself to take a longer look at the oracle card. A zing of fear shot through her spine and traveled to her fingers, her toes. Pictured was a close-up view of a young woman's face on a moss green background, her wide eyes clouded white—*blind*. It took everything in Birdie to keep her gaze upon the image long enough to read the heading.

The Seer.

Isn't that what Marcel had referred to her as during his little invocation? Bile rose in her throat.

"Birdie?" Dodge's voice was soft and comforting. She sat on the bench and patted the space next to her. "Look, I know I can be pretty in your face. It's just because I'm passionate. I'm sorry the cards upset you. I can put them away." Dodge made to scoop them up and return them to the deck.

"Wait." Birdie sighed, sat next to the musician, and crossed her arms over her stomach. She mulled over her next words before speaking again. "Dodge, what would you do if you couldn't be a musician anymore?"

Dodge raised an eyebrow at her and was quiet for some time. "My fire would dim." She stroked the strings on her guitar, letting each casual note ring out. When she finished, she looked out over the lawn, the setting sun reflecting in her eyes as she turned that gaze on Birdie. "Music is woven in my

DNA." Dodge held her hands over her heart. "Music is what fuels my soul. I can't imagine a scenario where I wouldn't find a way to express the rhythms and songs in my heart."

Birdie smiled sadly. "You're so...determined."

"I don't know how to be any other way." Dodge hugged her guitar to her and began a steady strum of sweet notes.

"I think I'm going blind."

Dodge's fingers slipped. Her melody ended abruptly and off key. She set the guitar back down, then repositioned herself on the bench with intense focus on Birdie yet didn't say anything.

The fears and feelings poured forth from Birdie. "My father went blind when I was a kid. It came on suddenly, some kind of aggressive form of macular degeneration. Apparently, it can run in the family. I thought I had more time. I'm about ten years younger than he was when it happened. It was very hard on our family. He lost his job, and my mother wasn't working at the time. But that's not the worst part..." She gripped the arm of the wicker bench and gulped, before turning to Dodge. "He started having these hallucinations. He was home all the time; I had to help guide him around until he could do it my memory. He would talk about seeing things, things that weren't there."

Dodge took up Birdie's hands in hers. "That must be terrifying."

Birdie nodded. "Dodge, I love photography like you love music. What am I going to do?"

She looked down, pensive. "What do *you* want to do?"

This took Birdie aback. Most people would jump to offer their thoughts and opinions, tell her to go to the doctor, to calm down. "I want to finish this residency and create my greatest work yet."

Dodge smirked, but this time it felt warm and supportive. She patted Birdie's hands and resumed a normal sitting position. "Well then, love, that's just what you'll do."

When Dodge got up, Birdie touched her arm. "Before we go inside...can you read my last card?" Birdie's eyes flicked to the third, unturned card on the table.

"Yes ma'am, we can." Dodge sat opposite of Birdie across the coffee table, kneeling. She touched the final card reverently, then revealed it: a burly, bearded man in flannel with an axe over his shoulder, an accomplished grin on his face. A felled tree lay in the background. "Oh wow. You've gotten the Woodcutter."

Birdie perched on the edge of her seat. "Is that good?"

Dodge cocked her head to the side, her chestnut hair flowing over her left shoulder. "I'd say so." She took the card and pressed it into Birdie's hands. "Take it. Vision or no, I have a feeling that you'll cut down any obstacle in the way of your dreams."

As Birdie followed Dodge back into the mansion, she pocketed the card. Dark days may be in her future, but she pledged to pull it out anytime she wanted a reminder to embrace the last light she might have left.

12

A week had passed since Dodge read Birdie's oracle cards. Birdie quickly fell into a comfortable and pleasant daily ritual. Breakfast with the gang: Adriana cooking something scrumptious, Tom already out and about, Dodge cracking jokes, and Marcel taking to writing down poems for them to read since his voice was still on the fritz as he recovered from his cold. The feeling of home she'd encountered at the Weeping Willow had only deepened since then, especially as she hadn't experienced any further strange visions or difficulties with her eyesight. It allowed her room to breathe, to focus on her art. Besides, she'd resolved to visit an optometrist once she was done with the residency. Maybe the whole thing had been a false alarm, brought on by the stress of a new place and people, and she'd never receive the diagnosis her father did.

After breakfast each day, Birdie made a trek she could now do with her eyes shut, to the nest cradled in the arms of the great willow tree and back. Her boots had worn the red dirt along the trail smooth. She'd done her research and discovered the pair of birds were, in fact, mourning doves. They parented together, each taking shifts sitting on their two eggs. Based on the articles she'd read and the amount of time it'd been since she'd first spotted the eggs, Birdie expected them to hatch very soon—it only took about two weeks from the dove laying the eggs to the baby birds hatching. Each morning, she grabbed her camera, bag, and mug of coffee, eager to capture the moment the birds broke free of their shells. It would be a spectacular set of images for her collection.

Bird-watching took her till about lunch, when she would have to tear herself away from the nest and tree to answer her rumbling stomach. The afternoon was usually set aside for more bird watching, photo editing, or hanging out with Dodge. They'd often sit together on the front porch, cooling themselves with the hand-carved fans that Tom had made for them and pulling oracle cards for each other.

Today she found herself hunched on her plush comforter in her bed and editing a couple shots of the way the roots of the Weeping Willow infiltrated the nearby creek bed. At first she hadn't realized what had caused the red clay to go white. She studied her screen, drawn in by the delicate offshoots of the winding roots.

"Birdie?" Adriana opened the door and poked her head in.

Birdie blinked hard and stretched. "Oh, hi, Adriana. Come on in. What's up?"

Adriana dipped her head sheepishly and entered. "I'm sorry. I knocked, but I guess you didn't hear me."

"Ha, yeah, sometimes I get like that when I'm really in the mode." Birdie closed her laptop and set it aside. "Goodness, my eyes are burning. I needed to take a break. I'm glad you stopped by."

Adriana leaned against the bed. She clapped her hands together, perking up. "*Excelente.* Perhaps you might be up for taking a longer break then?"

Birdie swung her legs over the side of the bed and laughed. "Sure. What you got in mind?"

"Well," Adriana said, pacing over the throw rug, her excited energy infectious. "As you know, I've been trying out recipes from the book I found in the mansion. I've finally managed to collect all the local ingredients for this one dessert recipe—"

"Say no more." Birdie hopped up. "I'm in."

"I thought you might be. Let's go." Adriana headed for the door.

Through the shared bathroom, from her bed in the adjoining room, Dodge hollered. "Hey, what's on the menu for tonight?"

"I thought you were taking a nap." Birdie chuckled.

"Mind your own beeswax, woman. This is important business." Dodge feigned a serious tone but couldn't hide her ever-present spirit of jest.

Adriana clucked her tongue. "*Chicas,* hush, and I will tell you." When Birdie and Dodge quieted their laughter, Adriana spoke. "Tonight's dinner will include a hush-puppies appetizer, fried green tomato sliders with a side of okra, as well as old fashioneds, and chilled sweet tea. Dessert will remain a surprise." She winked at Birdie.

"You good?" Birdie asked.

"Yeah." Dodge yawned loudly and put her head back down on her pillow. "I'm good. Y'all have fun baking."

Once in the kitchen, Adriana introduced Birdie

to the spread of ingredients she'd laid out for the recipe. The table overflowed with a huge bowl of plump peaches, bags of flour and sugar, a carton of milk, cinnamon, vanilla, baking powder, and salt. Birdie picked up a rotund root and scrunched her nose. "Ginger, right?"

"Sí." Adriana handed Birdie an apron peppered with tiny hand-painted wildflowers before donning her own, hers freckled with pastel-blue dots.

Birdie walked down the long counter to get a closer examination of an ingredient she didn't immediately recognize. Nestled next to the now-very-familiar jar of Orchard Hill honey, sat a small glass sauce bowl filled with fine red dust. "What's this?"

Adriana put a hand on her hip, proud. "That is red Georgian clay. Oh, don't frown at me like that. I've sifted it. It's perfectly fine in small doses and will give a lovely color to our ice cream."

"Yum, ice cream." Birdie tried for enthusiasm yet sincerely hoped that Adriana could work her magic so that it didn't taste gritty. "So is that what we're making then?"

"That's part of it." Adriana lifted the yellowing recipe book and traced her finger along the words on the open page. "Peach cobbler with honey willow ice cream."

Birdie had to admit it sounded delicious, and Adriana had yet to fail to deliver on taste. "Wait. Did you say—"

Adriana produced several ten-inch-long strips of a flimsy wood material. "I wanted to make this dessert earlier, but it has very specific instructions about collecting and drying the willow tree bark." She inspected the strips. "I believe they're finally ready."

Edging closer, Birdie ran her finger along one. "Where did you get these from? Tell me you didn't..."

Adriana pressed the bark to her chest and averted her eyes. Her words came faster and more heavily accented. "I mean, it's the only tree in the area in good enough condition to use. Plus, I thought it only proper for my willow-inspired culinary masterpiece to come from the—"

"*The Weeping Willow.*" Birdie drew in a sharp breath, then bit her lip. Everything had been going so smoothly, so well. This felt like kicking a dormant hornet's nest. "Adriana—"

Adriana held up a stern finger. "No. Don't start with the spooky this and silly superstition that. *This*"—she shook the bundle of bark at Birdie—"*this* is my future. Did you know that the willow bark has medicinal qualities?" She pointed a slender finger at the jar of honey on the counter. "That too. Can you imagine? An irresistible southern dessert that boasts healing properties and communing with the dead. People will travel from all over the country—no, the world—for something like that. A truly unique experience."

Birdie pressed her lips into a fine line, knowing that it wouldn't hold back her next words. "I want to support you. I really do. But how can you sell that when you don't believe in ghosts?"

The chef rolled her eyes, not so much in mockery of Birdie, it seemed, but in exhaustion of the question, as if this wasn't the first time this point was made to her. "*Palomita,* you're missing the point. *I* don't have to believe anything. It's all about what they believe, what they *crave.*"

Unwilling to antagonize Adriana further, Birdie

assisted Adriana in preparing the dessert. This didn't prevent Birdie from flinching each time Adriana's knife chopped another section of willow bark.

Waving the knife in the air, Adriana mused. "Besides, the medicinal properties of the bark are commonly held knowledge. They say it's like aspirin. I just hope it helps Marcel's voice some." Adriana set the knife down on the cutting board and stroked her throat. "Me too actually. I think I might be coming down with whatever Marcel had." She pinched the bridge of her nose. "It's strange. I don't feel stuffed up, but it's like my sinuses are clogged. Usually I can taste and smell the most minute elements of my meals. Yet lately, it's been a bit muted."

Birdie simply nodded at that and started washing, peeling, and slicing peaches as instructed. The next hour passed in relative quiet as Birdie didn't feel like engaging and Adriana was focused on ensuring everything was prepared to her liking. Birdie kept her mind off her unease by trying to enjoy working with her hands and getting a break from the computer screen. She watched Adriana move about, timing, measuring, stirring, and directing like some sort of orchestra conductor. It was mesmerizing, and time moved swiftly.

Before she knew it, Adriana was setting a sample of steaming peach cobbler in front of her and scooping a heaping portion of ice cream on top. Tinted red from the clay, the ice cream slid across the hot serving of cobbler as it melted on contact. Adriana opened the utensil drawer, pulled out two spoons, and handed one to Birdie. Birdie held up her hand to refuse. "Oh, I'm not hungry yet. I can wait till later, after dinner."

"Don't be silly. We need to taste test it. With my

taste buds being out of sorts, I could really use your opinion on it." Adriana extended the spoon again. "Please."

Birdie swallowed. Her mouth watered at the smell of the warm peaches and softening cream. Was she being silly? She wanted to support Adriana. She forced a smidge of excitement onto her face and snagged the spoon. "You're right. What good is going to all this trouble baking it if we're not going to try it?"

Together they filled their spoons with equal portions of ice cream and cobbler. Birdie attempted to take less of the ice cream, but Adriana's nostrils flared when she noticed, so Birdie got a healthy helping of each. Clammy from the heat of the oven and moving around, Birdie's heart fluttered right before she put the bite into her mouth.

The coolness of the ice cream hit her first, followed shortly by the warm, gooey peaches. Nothing was gritty about this dessert; it was smooth, exciting, and unique. A delightful bitterness, which she assumed could be attributed to the willow bark, crashed into the sweetness of the honey.

Birdie closed her eyes, savoring the flavors. She put her spoon down. "Adriana, that was breathtaking. I didn't know food could taste like that."

Adriana didn't respond. All Birdie heard was the clink of the spoon on the dish, again and again, frenzied. Birdie opened her eyes, her nerves rattled by the fervor in which Adriana ate more and more of the dessert. Birdie reached out and looped her fingers around Adriana's wrist. Only then did the chef look up.

Utter horror filled her features in such a manner as Birdie had never seen on the woman's face.

Adriana always had a pleasant sort of mask about her features, happy enough, excited enough, never any truly exaggerated emotion. But this—she was *terrified*.

"What's wrong?" Birdie still held Adriana's wrist.

Adriana gently removed Birdie's grip from her hand. The horror melted away from her eyes, her forehead, her mouth, and reformed into the pleasant mask. She picked up the nearly empty dish and began washing it in the sink, her back to Birdie. "It's fine. I'm sure it's just a cold. That's all it is."

13

The bitterness of the honey willow ice cream lingered on Birdie's tongue as she stood in the parlor that led off the left of the foyer, connected through the formal dining room, and circled back around to the kitchen along with the dining table they used more often. Like many of the other rooms in the mansion, this one had floor-to-ceiling windows framed by even longer cream drapes that pooled on the floorboards. She drew them shut against the growing darkness outside and flicked on three of the Tiffany stained-glass lamps on various polished wooden side tables scattered throughout the room. They created a soft warmth to the space, which was welcome, yet cast oblong shadows on the Willa Cromwell portraits covering the far wall.

As she waited alone for the others to join her for after-dinner drinks and conversation before bed, Birdie positioned herself in front of the unlit fireplace. Black splotches charred the beige stone in unruly streaks like wicked starbursts. The largest of the Cromwell portraits hung above the mantle, not a particularly interesting specimen: a plain face, plainly painted. Birdie was happy the artist who'd created it managed to dampen Willa's signature, soul-searing stare.

Down the hall, glasses clinked as Adriana prepared old fashioneds and tea for everyone. Dodge sang upstairs, having decided to take a quick shower while Marcel took the intervening time to write in his room. Tom made no noise as usual and would probably show up in the same manner until he made a disapproving grunt at something someone said. Birdie smiled, moving to the series of portraits cascading down the wall to the right of the fireplace, musing how only after a week, she'd grown accustomed to, and even frequently enjoyed, her resident artist companions.

Circumventing one of the two great wingback chairs that guarded either side of the fireplace, she dragged her fingers lightly across the velvety evergreen upholstery, then began to inspect the portraits more closely. Typically Adriana would've joined her by now, providing a welcome distraction from the shuddersome decor she'd always done her best to ignore. She worried that after their baking complications earlier, Adriana was stalling to avoid her.

Most of the portraits clouding the foyer and bleeding into the parlor consisted of some variation of paint: oil, water, acrylic. Others were done in mixed media of the most hair-raising quality, and Birdie avoided those no matter how bored she found herself. But here, on this wall, hidden behind a tall lamp nearer to the corner, she spied a small, five-by-eight-inch frame that she hadn't taken a closer look at before.

The only one of its kind in the house, near as she could tell, it held an actual photograph. In the hollow of a weeping willow's shadow, an image of

Willa Cromwell gazed out at the camera, dead-eyed yet somehow piercingly judgmental. Her mousy brown hair hung limply, her mouth a simple line with down-turned corners, the shape of her nose forgotten as soon as Birdie looked away. Unsettling as it was to see the depictions of Willa Cromwell in portraits, seeing a real-life picture of her was upending and disorienting. The deceased benefactress both hit a nerve of self-doubt but also left the impression of someone you should be able to recall yet can't, shifting the answer away right as it's sought.

Spots floated across her field of vision, and Birdie scratched at her dry eyes. The parlor tilted, and she gripped the back of the chair for stability. When the feeling subsided, she forced her attention back to the photograph. Looking over her shoulder to make sure no one was coming, she unhooked the frame from the wall and pulled the string to turn on the floor lamp a few inches from her.

In the back of her mind, she'd long been wondering why her discipline was one of the chosen five for the residency. Here was clear evidence, aside from the instructions in her will, that Willa's passion and involvement in the arts extended beyond the paintings they'd seen in the mansion. Birdie glanced up at the ceiling, imagining what strange creations might be sealed within the madwoman's room. Her eyelid twitched at what her imagination conjured, suddenly feeling very cold for the damp heat in the room.

Turning her attention back to the photograph, she flipped over the frame to inspect the back, mostly with the intention of opening it and looking at what was on the reverse side of the image. Often, photographs contained more information there—

the date, the location, the artist's name, the subject. Anything to give her more information about Willa's work with another photographer. Before she could open it, something caught her eye that gave her pause.

A line of red paint.

Across the back of the frame's stiff board lay a single three-inch line of red paint, hastily done with unclean edges. The thumping of feet barreling down the staircase caused Birdie to lose her hold on the picture, and she dropped it.

It clattered loudly on the wood. She sucked in a deep breath, waiting for the glass to shatter. When it didn't, she quickly scooped up the frame and with shaky hands, replaced it on the wall. She was straightening it when she heard someone enter the parlor behind her.

"I thought you couldn't stand looking at those creepy portraits." Birdie came around the wingback chair as Dodge hopped over the back of the matching, button-studded couch and made herself comfortable. "Don't you just feel like this place has got to be haunted?"

Before Birdie could answer, Adriana walked in, carrying a large silver tray packed with lowball glasses sloshing with amber liquid. "Ay, díos mio, not this talk again." She set the tray on the coffee table in the center of the room, lifted a drink to her mouth, and made a face when she swallowed. "Even alcohol?" She pursed her lips and held the glass up in a toast to the portrait above the mantle. "I think we've discussed *Señorita* Cromwell and her vile behavior enough, haven't we?"

Birdie's eyes widened, and Dodge stifled a giggle as Marcel, a mischievous glint in his eyes, tiptoed into the room behind Adriana and blew softly on the nape of her neck. Adriana shrieked and spun around, coming face to face with Marcel, who feigned innocence. Her frustration crescendoed in an irritated scream as she cocked her arm and threw her glass over the threshold into the foyer. It nearly missed Tom's head as he arrived, shattering in a shower of sparkling shards and bourbon against one of Willa's portraits before raining to the floor.

Everyone fell silent. The only sounds were the steady *drip, drip, drip* of the ruined drink.

Tom growled, stormed toward Marcel, and heaved him up by his lapels. "Leave her alone."

Marcel could only make small squeaks, holding his hands up in defense. Dodge was on her feet, soon followed by Birdie, who gathered near the two men. But it was Adriana who first spoke. "Put him down." Her stern voice gave no room for disagreement.

"But—" Tom only had eyes for Adriana as he lowered Marcel to his feet yet did not let him go.

"I don't need you to save me, Tom." Adriana reached for another drink, shook her head, not taking it, and exited the parlor, heading upstairs. If she saw the hurt and confusion on Tom's face, she didn't appear to care. "I'm going to bed. *Buenos noches.*"

With that, she disappeared up the staircase. As soon as she was out of sight, each of them reacted. Marcel shrugged and settled into the couch with a drink, Tom started cleaning up the mess, and Dodge shared a concerned look with Birdie.

Birdie sighed. "I know; that's not like her. I have an idea what's bothering her. Let me go try to talk to her."

"Want me to come?" Dodge asked.

Birdie brushed by her, touching her on the shoulder. "Nah, thank you. Too many of us and she might feel like we're ganging up on her."

Dodge tipped an imaginary hat. "Yes, ma'am, makes sense. Good luck, love." Dodge joined Marcel on the couch.

Birdie entered the foyer and stopped by Tom, who kneeled on the floor, cleaning. "You want some help?"

"No," he snapped.

"Okay." Birdie dawdled a few moments, hoping he might change his mind or talk to her, even if it was only a couple more words. For him, that would equate to a whole conversation. She watched him mop up the drink with a hand towel and noticed the liquid had a ruddier tinge than it should. Birdie crouched next to him. "Hey, did you cut yourself?"

Tom paused and held out his hands, palms up. Indeed, a sliver of glass stuck out of his thumb. He tugged on it, and it slipped out. Blood pooled at the small wound. "Huh," he said with mild surprise.

Birdie held up a finger. "Ouch. I'll grab a bandage." She hurried off to the bathroom and came back quickly to apply it.

He batted her hand away. "I can do it. Go talk to her."

Birdie held his eyes briefly, then handed him the bandage. "You got it."

Comforted that everyone downstairs seemed as settled as they could be after the outburst, she made her way upstairs to Adriana's room. She was glad to give the chef some time to let her steam of emotions cool off before approaching her anyway. Birdie knocked softly on the door. "Adriana? Can I come in?"

A sizable pause answered her. Perhaps she'd already fallen asleep?

"Sí, palomita. You may enter." Adriana no longer sounded angry. Rather, her words carried sadness and lacked the usual cheer and enthusiasm.

Only a single lamp lit the room, a cozy spotlight on the woman curled up on her bed, her arms around her knees. Birdie came in and sat down when Adriana waved a hand for her to sit next to her. Taking a page from Dodge, Birdie didn't rush into speaking, guessing that Adriana might open up in the space she made for her to talk.

Adriana blew her bangs out of her eyes. They were red-rimmed and watery. "I know you take this stuff—these 'precautions'—more seriously, but you know it's not real, right?" She dug her nails into the skin of her forearms. Birdie wanted to reach out, to loosen her grip before she hurt herself. Adriana turned a heated glare onto Birdie. "Ghosts aren't *real*. You've got to know that?"

Birdie faced the door, pensive. Adriana wanted to hear that she agreed with her. Yet Birdie's experiences and her desires were two separate animals. Birdie started slowly. "What I know is…there are things in this world that I can't begin to understand. I can't say that there are no ghosts." Adriana opened her mouth to interrupt, but Birdie held up her hand to stay her. "Nor can I say with confidence that ghosts exist. So I err on the side of caution."

Adriana sniffled and cleared her throat. Birdie snatched the box of tissues off the nightstand for her. After she blew her nose, Adriana spoke. "Whether they exist or not, we all came here for a reason—to create our artistic masterpieces. This means the difference between being a household restaurant name and head chef and being a nobody in the back of a kitchen, begging to be a sous chef. You all can let silly little superstitions and perfectly explainable occurrences stop you from pursuing your dreams, but I'm not going to let *anything* stop me."

Birdie turned toward Adriana and held up her pinkie finger. "Now with that, I couldn't agree more. Let's do what we came here to do."

Adriana stared at Birdie's pinkie-promise offer for a long moment. Then she flashed her teeth in a wide grin. She hooked pinkies with Birdie, shook her hand, and they both hugged.

14

Eagerness soared through Birdie's heart with the breaking dawn. She woke early, showered, and packed her camera bag before Adriana had even gotten up and started breakfast in the kitchen. The mansion was quiet and still as she made a quick cup of tea to go; even the portraits of Willa appeared to approve her early start.

After leaving a note for the others on her whereabouts, she shut the double doors with the softest of clicks and took a big breath of fresh air once on the porch. Clean, dewy, and with a hint of the minerals and greenery, the air soothed her. The sun shone pink and purple along the scattered clouds on the horizon. Birds chirped their good mornings to the rising sun.

Birdie spotted the oracle deck on the table, left out by Dodge the day prior. She gathered the cards, shuffling them, and closed her eyes. Remembering how Dodge pulled cards, she fanned out the deck and let her hand waver until she felt compelled—this was the right card. She'd seen Dodge sometimes do this, ask a question to herself in the mornings, and only draw one card for the day. Her spirits high, she figured her card would only energize her further.

She flipped it over: *Nature's Bond.*

A big smile spread across her face. She sprung to her feet and started along the path to the Weeping Willow. Everything pointed to today being the day the mourning doves would hatch from their eggs.

Rays of sunlight spilled through the trees, filtered like dazzling fingers to wave hello to her. Birdie passed the leaning shed, then diverted to walk along the creek. Lost in her own excitement, she nearly missed the hunched figure in the creek bed ahead of her. He was unmistakable in his fading black tank top.

"Tom?" she called out.

He didn't turn.

Usually she started her mornings later than him, and if she did happen upon him during her excursions, he was so busy collecting organic bits and bobs for his sculpture—which he'd let no one lay eyes on for the whole week he's been working on it —that he merely mumbled salutations to her and carried on. She couldn't recall a time she'd seen him sitting or resting, unless it was at the dinner table. And even then, he gave the impression of being antsy to get back to work.

"Tom? Are you okay?" Birdie's stomach fluttered, and her heart sped. Her muscles told her to turn heel and run.

Something wasn't right.

Ignoring every instinct in her body, Birdie continued at a slow pace toward Tom, doing her best to make her footsteps loud enough on the red clay so she didn't sneak up on him. Despite their rocky start, she'd become fond of Tom; they'd developed a sort of kinship, being the only two of the residents to originate from southern Georgia itself. She couldn't abandon him if something was wrong, even though she was frightened.

His back was to her as he sat on the creek bed, his knees drawn up and legs spread. His shoulders worked, ratcheting back and forth, back and forth. Perhaps he was concentrating on sculpting something small, a component of his larger work?

Birdie rounded him, thinking it best not to disturb him if she could avoid it. Startling a big man like that was unwise. She skirted thick, twisted roots near the edge of the bed and when she was clear of them, moved in a wide circle to get a better look at him.

She stopped dead in her tracks.

Her mouth opened to scream, but nothing came out. Tom held a whittling knife, its sharp, two-inch blade set in a wood-grained handle, the perfect length to rest in his palm. The object of his sculpting, however, wasn't a piece of wood—it was his own skin. He slashed, paused, dug his nails into the skin, then slashed again. Crimson flooded from the wounds and blended into the red clay around him.

When shock melded into numbness, Birdie realized tears streamed down his face in dirty maroon streaks and his mouth drew up crookedly in distress. Still, he did not stop.

Birdie looked around at the landscape surrounding them, devoid of anyone to help her help him. She gritted her teeth, set her bag aside behind her, and placed her hands out in front of her as she approached him. "Tom," she said, full of caution. "Tom, please stop."

Tom didn't acknowledge her until she stayed his

hands. He let her take the knife, then displayed his wounds to her. His pupils were wide and swallowing in their vulnerability. "I can't feel. I can't feel *anything*." Tears again pooled and flowed like a silent waterfall down his blood-smeared cheeks. "Birdie, what's wrong with me?"

Hearing her name snapped her out of her fear. She took the bottom of her shirt and used the whittling knife to shred two long strips. Then she wrapped them around each of Tom's hands.

She helped him to his feet, then guided him to the path, to the mansion. The whole way back, she held her arms around him as best she could, the giant of a man helpless as a child in her care, shivering and leaning into her comfort.

What was happening to them?

15

A sourness curled inside Birdie's stomach and refused to leave. Her bright outlook for the day a distant memory, she set up her tripod at the Weeping Willow to assess the status of the mourning doves' eggs.

After she'd helped Tom inside the house, Adriana and Marcel aided her in making sure the bleeding had stopped, he was properly bandaged, and at last, was resting in his room. A faint snore let them know he'd fallen asleep. The wounds had looked worse than they really were, which was something to be thankful for. Yet his behavior was disconcerting. She'd wanted to stay at the mansion to help watch over him, but Adriana had all but kicked her out, telling her to change her shirt and stick to her pinkie promise or else.

She'd dragged her feet all the way to the Weeping Willow, where she now stood. Adriana was right, she spied through her camera lens—the first egg already had an inch-long crack in it. If she hadn't come out now, she'd have missed her chance. She snapped a few pictures in quick succession, then stepped back, pacing. Birdie ran her hand through her hair, her nerves singing with stress. She'd just get these pictures now and then go back and insist they take Tom to the hospital. They all should go, really, take a break from Willow Creek Mansion for a night at the very least.

Resolved in her decision, she squinted through the camera and observed one of the mourning doves—the father, she believed—helping the baby push through the shell with its beak and teasing the opening farther. Grit irritated Birdie's eyes, and she rubbed them to get relief from the parched itch, not recalling any particular gusts of wind that could've kicked up clay dust.

When the parent dove flew off with the eggshell, which Birdie knew from her research was to prevent infection and keep predators from finding the babies, she seized her opportunity. Unhooking the camera from the tripod, she snuck closer for a better vantage point. Climbing a bent root, she perched and zoomed in.

She blinked several times, thinking what she saw might be the result of clouding from her dry eyes. An ache radiated from deep within her temples. Her mind had difficulty registering what was in front of her.

A cloud passed overhead, blotting out the sun and shrouding her in darkness. Birdie inched closer to the nest, her breath held, anxiously raising the camera for a shot—*the shot* that would make or break her career. When the cloud cleared, a brutal ray of light highlighted the newborn bird in summery technicolor.

Birdie gasped.

Her foot slipped on the root, the camera tumbling out of her grasp. It landed hard on the ground, the lens cracking. As the camera crashed, the baby dove, agitated by the sound, jumped out of the nest.

Birdie, operating on sheer instinct, lunged forward and caught the tiny bird before it fell to its death. She trembled, her knees crying out from landing on the packed dirt and roots near the trunk of the Weeping Willow. She'd bit her tongue and felt certain it bled, if the metallic taste on her tongue was any indication.

The dove's talons tickled her palms, and its wet, goopy feathers repulsed her. It chirped angrily at her. With trepidation, she peered inside her hands at the newly born baby bird.

It had no eyes.

Where its eyes were supposed to be were simply dark, empty hollow sockets—voids that somehow still watched her. The dove pecked her viciously with its beak, drawing blood in tiny pinpricks.

Birdie thought she would be sick. She unloaded the horrid thing back into its nest. Its twin had broken free from its shell, and together the hatchlings cried up at her, eyeless. Birdie's vision blackened at the edges. The sounds of the forest around her quieted until all she heard were the chicks' insistent chirps. Birdie was rooted to the spot. The wind kicked up through the Weeping Willow's ample emerald leaves and the chirps morphed and blended with whispering wind until all Birdie heard was a single word.

"See, see, see, see, see."

She scrambled backwards, abandoning her camera and equipment. The word chased her all the way down the path. Birdie ran until her calves screamed and her breath came in ragged gasps, not daring to stop until she reached the mansion's porch steps. She desperately wanted to pursue her photography career, but nothing was worth this. She'd find another way. Nothing could keep her at Willow Creek another night.

16

Her suitcase bounced from the force of Birdie slamming it onto the bed. She slung open her dresser drawers and tossed her clothes into it, shoving them in as fast as she could. Then she turned her attention to rounding up her other possessions in the room into her backpack: books, laptop, sunglasses, etc.

As she darted into the bathroom to collect her toiletries, Dodge opened the opposite door. "Birdie, you got a second? I've got to talk to you about something." The singer, distant and distracted, braced one arm on the counter and tugged at her earlobe with the other. "Uh, what you doing there?"

Birdie froze, holding an armful of lotion, shampoo, and body wash. Dodge raised her eyebrows, puzzlement evident on her face. What was she doing? She couldn't go and leave everyone else here. Birdie added her toiletries to her already stuffed backpack. Dodge followed her into her room.

Birdie inhaled, lifting her hands up with the breath, then pushed them down as she exhaled. When she felt a small measure of calm return, she addressed Dodge. "Marcel has almost completely lost his voice. Adriana can't taste or smell anything she cooks." Birdie ticked off on her fingers as she spoke. "Tom can't feel. And I..." She rubbed her eyes again. "Don't even get me started on the birds." She placed her hands on Dodge's shoulders. "Something is *seriously* wrong here. I'm not crazy. We have to get out of here. We have to get everyone out of here."

Dodge focused on Birdie's mouth as she spoke. Birdie held her breath while she waited for the woman's reaction to what she'd said. She imagined anyone else might tell her to calm down, a perfectly logical explanation could be made, it was all coincidence. But Dodge's advice was one she'd grown to appreciate, and she felt exposed, waiting for her thoughts on the matter. Dodge licked her lips and blinked, her eyes flicking to the suitcase on the bed. "You're completely right. Something is wrong here."

The tension that had strung Birdie's shoulder up like a marionette suddenly dropped away. She plopped down on the bed by her overflowing pile of clothes. "What?"

Dodge joined her on the bed. "I'm not blind." When Birdie flinched, Dodge patted her hand. "Sorry, poor choice of words, love. What I'm saying is that I've noticed it too. Things are getting out of hand. But are we sure leaving is going to fix it?"

"Well, what do you suggest?" Birdie got up, then sat down. "I can't do nothing."

Dodge smirked. "Did I say that? No, I think we should get to the bottom of this. Besides, I'm not sure the others will leave unless we have more compelling evidence. At least, not—"

"Adriana. No, you're right." Birdie went to the window, drawing the curtains closed against the early evening crickets, cringing at their increasing chorus of chirps. "Maybe there's something in Willa's room that can give us an idea of what's going on?"

A knock on the door interrupted them.

"Come in?" Birdie tilted her head.

Marcel sauntered in, a fountain pen and exquisite journal in hand. He held up a finger, then used Birdie's nightstand for support while he wrote. When he was done, he held it up for them both to see.

Oh, honey, we already tried that. It's sealed to the nines.

Birdie looked questioningly at Dodge, who shrugged sheepishly and cracked a tiny grin. "Even my lock picking skills were no match."

Birdie sighed, leaning against the wall, one foot propped up. Quiet filled the room while they thought. Then Birdie tapped her head back against the wall and pushed off.

She couldn't believe she'd forgotten about them.

Without a word, she moved around the bed and past Dodge and Marcel, who both furrowed their brows while Birdie opened the nightstand drawer.

With hesitant triumph, she presented the ring of keys she'd found by the shed within the first days of arriving at Willow Creek. "These might work."

17

"Shhh...be quiet, she's going to hear you." Birdie huddled with Dodge and Marcel in front of the grand double doors in the middle of the upstairs hall. She fingered through the keys, trying to guess which of the twenty-some on the ring to try first. They'd all retired to their rooms for the evening and made the plan to meet here when they could safely assume that Adriana and Tom had fallen asleep for the night. But Adriana's room was so close by that Birdie imagined every creak in the old mansion to be the chef emerging to chastise them for their ridiculousness.

"Just pick a key, love," Dodge said, way above a whisper and standing tall like she had nothing to hide.

Birdie chuffed and threw her an irritated look. The light from the foyer, left on each night in case someone needed to get a drink of water from the kitchen or something, wasn't enough to beat back the stretchy shadows in the hall. She supposed she could test every key in the lock, but that could make a lot of noise. There had to be a way to determine which would be the most likely to open Willa Cromwell's overly ornate doors.

A tiny beacon of light illuminated the lock and key ring. From over Birdie's left shoulder, Marcel pointed the flashlight.

"Thank you," Birdie mouthed. Holding up the keys, doing her level best to not let them clink too loudly as they shifted around the ring, she examined them for differences. From what Birdie knew about Willa... Would it be an equally ornate key to match the doors? Would it be the hefty one or the delicately thin one?

Birdie, quickly becoming familiar with each of them, stopped. Her spine tingled with a mixture of dread and anticipation. "Marcel," she whispered. "Can you bring the light a little closer?"

Every single key head included a curved *C* inlaid within the filagree—all except one. She polished the bronze in tiny circles, then revealed it to the others. Willow branches twined around in two great swoops forming a distinct *W*.

"This must be it." Birdie made eye contact with Dodge, then Marcel, each of whom nodded encouragingly toward the door. On bended knee, Birdie faced the lock. Marcel's flashlight shone on the gleaming wood door, and Birdie wondered whether it had been carved from a local willow tree. She'd never really stopped to study its designs. Who'd want to linger at Willa's door?

Now it was all she could see. Sweat trickled down her back as she gaped upward at the imposing artwork above her. Where the doors met, they split down the heart of an enormous willow tree that had an eerie resemblance to the Weeping Willow. Within its branches, the silhouettes meandered and fused into more than just great leaves. They swerved one way to outline diving doves, another formed a scowling fox, and another a long-eared rabbit. The more Birdie looked, the more entranced she became, finding diminutive cicadas clinging to the tree trunk, so finely done she marveled at the craftsmanship. She wondered if Tom had examined the sculpting and why he'd never mentioned its beauty. Along the bottom panel, a creek so vivid it appeared as if the water truly flowed held her attention so long that Dodge tapped her shoulder.

Birdie licked her dry lips, wiping the beading sweat from her forehead, and she slid the key into the lock. The click echoed down the hall, and she scrunched her shoulders. When neither of the two sleeping residents investigated, she nudged open the doors.

After treading forward with care onto a woven rug, Dodge and Marcel closed the doors behind them. Birdie, with the help of Marcel's guiding light, found a light switch to the right on the wall. She flicked it.

A grand candelabra chandelier came to life above the center of the room. A heavy layer of dust-coated, discolored sheets were thrown over the myriad of objects in the room. Birdie could guess the biggest one in the back by the windows might be a four-poster bed. The others perhaps were wardrobes, dressers, and the like. But the strangest, which kept her feet rooted to the spot like a statue, trembling, were five covered figures about her height, evenly spaced in a wide semicircle around the presumed bed.

"What in tarnation?" Dodge stepped closer, but Birdie grabbed her arm.

"Careful. We don't know what we're dealing with." Yet Birdie didn't have a plan, and the look on Dodge's face told her she knew it. Birdie jumped when Marcel tapped her shoulder. "Sorry."

He lifted his journal. *We're with you, little bird.*

Marcel wrapped an arm around her, and Dodge looped another around her waist. The three of them stared down the troubling, unknown things in front of them. Comforted in the fact that none had moved of their own accord, Birdie felt reassured that whatever lay underneath weren't people.

At least, no one alive. She shivered with the urge to back out of the room and slam the doors shut forever.

No, they needed to figure out what was going on and whether it had anything to do with Willa Cromwell and her terrible invocation of passion fifty years ago.

Birdie left the comfort of Dodge and Marcel, motioning for them to stay back. She approached the first figure, farthest to the left. On leaden feet, she reached it and lifted tentative fingers. What could be underneath, she could only guess. Surely, it mustn't be that dreadful if the people who came after Willa, who administrated the grant and residency and tended to the mansion, had covered it. Yet it dawned on her: she'd never met these people; she knew nothing about them and their nature.

She was starting to realize she'd made a lot of assumptions about Willow Creek Mansion that she couldn't be so sure of now. Everything in her still wanted to turn tail and run far, far away. She opened and balled her hand into a fist a couple of times, the tips of her fingers not quite touching the draped fabric. Her strength would have to come from those who needed her—Tom's face, childlike, when he asked her what was wrong with him; the look of horror on Adriana's when she couldn't taste her own dessert; and Dodge and Marcel, who waited for her now, hoping she'd find answers. How she came to be the one they relied on, she had no idea. She was the one who sat nameless in corners at parties, too shy to mingle. She was the one who bristled at social encounters, even though it was a product of her own insecurities. She was no hero.

And yet...Birdie snapped her hand shut and tore off the sheet. Dust billowed around, the light catching the motes in pretty, little, cough-inducing sparkles. It stung her eyes. She shooed away what she could and stifled a cough. When the dust settled, she saw she'd revealed a tall wooden stand covered with a glass dome.

Under the cloche lay a simple tape recorder, well-preserved and disconcerting. Birdie beckoned Dodge and Marcel over. "What do you make of it?"

Dodge shrugged. "We already know this woman was a weirdo. Who knows?"

Marcel rolled his eyes, then straightened his vest. With care, he raised the dome, set it gently on the rug, and pressed play.

The cassette whirred and clicked. A minute passed. Two. They were deep into the third, Marcel's forefinger about to press pause, when they heard something, barely above a hoarse whisper.

"Seer..."

Tingling chills raced along Birdie's arms and neck. Dodge's eyes narrowed in confusion. Marcel stared hard at the recorder.

"Singer...speaker..."

Marcel's head snapped up, his eyes so wide his

pupils shone bone white. Birdie couldn't look away, though she desperately wanted to. She had enough fear coursing through her own veins that she couldn't carry the weight of Marcel's fear too.

"Sculptor...server..."

The tape hocked a looping click while they stood in stunned silence. Dodge finally pushed stop. Marcel pointed with ferocity at his throat.

Birdie returned the cloche and grimaced, swallowing over the sympathetic film in her throat. "I know. It's exactly what you said the other night. Even in the same order."

"Ready to check out the next one?" Dodge asked.

Birdie marveled at how impervious to being rattled the folk musician was. Pressing her palms to her eyes, Birdie psyched herself up. Four more. She could do it. How much worse could it get?

18

It turned out it could get worse. Much, *much* worse. The second cloche contained what at first appeared to be a bowl of decorative fruit. Upon closer inspection, the red clay bowl filled with carved peaches were clothed in canvases of stitched, hand painted skin.

"I really hope that's animal skin," Dodge said as she returned the glass dome.

"It's odd. It actually smelled a bit like real peaches, didn't it?" Birdie asked.

Marcel held up a note. *Next?*

Birdie sighed. "Yep. Though I'm not sure we're going to find any answers. I'm not even really sure what we're looking for."

Dodge tugged the cover off the third one. "Well, it doesn't hurt to finish, just to be sure."

Sidling up to the stand, Birdie frowned. "I'm not so sure."

Dodge raised her eyebrows. "Huh?"

"Nothing." In front of them rested a wooden box about the size of a mailbox. On one side, a round hole opened to the darkness within. Both Dodge and Marcel looked at Birdie. "What? Nuh uh, nope, no way."

"What if there's a clue in there?" Dodge laughed, but Birdie could tell her nerves were getting to her by the way she pushed her hair back. "It can't bite, right? I mean, it's been closed up in here forever."

Birdie squared off with the box and wondered if Willa's sensory deprivation box looked like a bigger version of this. The idea of sticking her hand in there made her skin crawl. She gritted her teeth. "We've come this far, haven't we?"

The lines on Marcel's forehead deepened with concern as Birdie slid her hand inside inch by inch. Nothing but damp air touched her. She lowered her palm slowly and made contact with a hard, uneven surface like tiny tiles. Digging into it, they slipped around, and she shrieked when a sharp one poked her.

Dodge was at her side immediately, cradling Birdie's wrist. The object stuck out of Birdie's skin, and Dodge plucked it out, the half-moon indent welling with blood. Birdie squinted at it as Dodge held it up to the light. "What is it?" Birdie asked.

"I don't know. It can't be what I think it is. Can it?" Dodge made a yucky face and set it on top of the box.

Marcel scribbled on his paper. *Honey, it's* exactly *what you think it is. That's a human fingernail. Ripped right from the bed.*

Birdie felt a dry heave coming on and leaned over. Dodge patted her on the back. "Okay, love. You took one for the team. I got the next one."

Rustling floated through the room as Dodge moved to the fourth stand. Birdie went to the door and pressed her ear against it. Nothing.

Marcel cocked his head at her. "I thought I heard something." Birdie rejoined them while Dodge freed the next item in Willa's macabre personal collection from its glass tomb. Birdie rubbed at her eyelids. "Ugh, this dust is killing me."

"This one isn't so bad." Dodge picked up a slender, ivory instrument with holes along the length of its hollow body. "I love a good recorder. I used to be really good at playing it until I picked up the guitar."

Dodge lifted one end to her lips. Birdie reached for her. "I don't think you should—"

Before Birdie could stop her, Dodge blew through the recorder. The sound that came out could only be described as a human being shrieking in absolute, torturous pain—so high pitched, desperate, and frightened that it bordered on animalistic. It reminded Birdie of the foxes' mating calls in the dead of night. She clamped her hands over her ears. "Stop!"

Dodge dropped the recorder, and it clattered on the rug. "Well, I definitely heard that." Though she joked, Birdie saw true terror breaking down Dodge's brave demeanor as the musician covered her mouth as if she'd been somehow unable to stop herself from playing the instrument.

Birdie stooped to pick it up, holding it far away from herself, while Marcel drolly underlined a note saying, *The entire state of Georgia heard that.*

"Correct me if I'm wrong, y'all, but I think this thing is carved from bone." Birdie showed it to them, and they each nodded. When she noticed Dodge crossing her arms like she was trying to keep herself from reaching for it again, Birdie replaced the recorder on its resting place on the stand. "Let's finish this last one. That sound might've woken up Adriana and Tom."

Dodge had gone pale, and Marcel didn't appear eager to interact with the fifth and final display, so Birdie stepped up once more. She eyed the row of four that had come before. Something about them, aside from their bloodcurdling components and sounds, bothered her in a way she couldn't quite put her finger on.

She proceeded with the same ritual, tearing off the sheet and lifting the cloche. Birdie pinched the bridge of her nose, puzzled. A plain red ribbon, about four inches wide and about five or six times as long, lay pooled on the wooden stand, making Birdie think of a pile of intestines, only because of the extraordinarily gross nature of Willa's other exhibits. Any other day, a normal day in a normal place, she'd have thought it pretty.

Dodge kneeled so she was face to face with it and poked it. "What's wrong with it?"

Birdie eased back, shaking her head. She pointed to the ribbon. "I think it's a blindfold."

Bewildered, Dodge followed Birdie's lead and backed away. "How do you figure?"

With nearly a life of its own, Birdie's pointer finger tracked each of the pieces in Willa's awful collection. "Speak...taste...touch...hear...and see."

Dodge placed a hand on Birdie's shoulder. Marcel's face fell, dismal. "I'm detecting a pattern," Dodge said. "But I don't see how this helps? Though the creep factor alone might be enough to convince everyone else we need to leave."

The wind picked up outside, whistling through the windowpanes. Glare from the faux candles in the chandelier settled in a hazy halo. Shadows from the branches outside crept into the room, slinking their way over a sheet across the way. Birdie squinted at it, blinked—a vision of the gnarled shade enclosing its spindly fingers over the cloth. All else in Willa's room receded into the background as Birdie drew toward the strange sighting.

"Birdie?" Dodge sounded so very far away.

Birdie's fingers twitched in dismissive response. The whistle of the wind pitched higher and only ceased its howling once she stood in front of the covered furniture gripped by shadows. She grasped the cloth, unveiling what lay hidden beneath for countless years.

The face of a frightened woman confronted her.

It took Birdie a moment to realize the face was her own. A mirror cast her reflection back to her, mounted on a massive vanity. Trailing scratches marred the gleaming surface. Birdie traced their outlines with her nails. The color and shape of her fingernails morphed from plainly buffed to red talons. By the time she registered what she thought she saw, her nails were again free of polish and cut short.

Closing her eyes, which she started to worry were not a source she could trust any longer, she clutched the underside of the vanity to ground herself. The pad of her left ring finger sensed a small circular outline. She depressed it, and a hidden drawer popped open. Birdie turned to Dodge and Marcel. "Hey, I found something."

19

Fireflies graced the humid night air, their glimmering on-again, off-again lanterns bobbing in the ocean of darkness in front of Willow Creek Mansion. Birdie, Dodge, and Marcel gathered on the porch. They opted to keep the porch lights off in case they disturbed Tom and Adriana, though that was out of an abundance of caution. This late in the night, bordering on the technicality of morning, tended to have that effect.

Dodge lit several squat, teal candles on the coffee table. Marcel lent Birdie his flashlight, then picked up one of the wooden fans Tom had carved to fan himself. Birdie couldn't tell whether it was hers with the sparrow or Dodge's with the rabbit. It didn't really matter, but it made the skin on the back of her neck crawl that she couldn't tell from a few feet away. The candles only provided so much light, she guessed.

Poor Tom. When would he be able to carve like that again, after what he'd done to his hands? She couldn't fathom that he would just do that to himself out of the blue, with no obvious reason. Each of them was being affected in a way that destroyed them the most, hampering the abilities they relied on to create their art, to express their passion.

Passion. Birdie caressed the cover of the leather-bound diary she'd found hidden in Willa's vanity. She opened it to the first page. In harsh cursive, she read, *This diary belongs to Willa Cromwell.* Everything pointed back to Willa. "Why did you bring us here?" Birdie whispered.

"What's it say?" Dodge asked, rather loudly.

Marcel tossed the musician a shrewd glare. He jotted down a note and handed it to Birdie. *My dear little bird, you may consider starting first with the end. That looks like a mighty fine volume, and I believe we're most interested in the finale.*

Birdie gave him his journal back. "Yeah, that's smart." She flipped to the last page that held writing from the cruel benefactress. Her eyes went wide at the bizarre scribbles and drawings that flashed by. On the last page, Willa had penned a crude image of a great willow tree in so hard a hand that the paper ran jagged. Underneath the trunk of the tree, hastily accomplished, Willa had written an inscription. "In death, I shall grow. In rebirth, I shall blossom," Birdie read aloud.

Dodge leaned forward from the bench and cupped her ear. "Come again?"

First swallowing hard over the lump in her throat, Birdie repeated the words. "What does it mean? That she really is dead?"

Dodge rearranged her sitting position on the long cushion, tucking her legs back and to the side. "It could be poetry. Song lyrics. Random words gathered for later creative use. We all do it, don't we?"

Marcel nodded. He mimed for Birdie to turn to the previous page in the diary.

When Birdie did so, her forefinger caught on the page's edge and sliced her skin. She hissed, drawing her finger back to her mouth. Then she inspected the stinging wound. Blood welled in the thin line and dripped onto the page. Her gaze traveled from her finger to the brilliant red spot. The blood was hyperreal, but all else on the page blurred into black wavy lines instead of words.

Dodge got up and sat down next to her. "You okay?"

"Huh?" Birdie felt dazed. She rubbed her temples with her middle fingers, taking care of the injured one. Her vision was definitely hindered. But if she were experiencing the early onset of macular degeneration, like her father, she should be having trouble with her central vision, not her peripheral. This was the opposite, as if her good vision was being chipped away from the outside in. She pushed the diary over to Dodge. "Can you read it?"

"Okay." Dodge scanned the text. Every third line, she'd gasp or make a worried noise in the back of her throat.

Marcel whacked her lightly with the wooden fan.

"Jeez, chill out. This cursive is literally from hell." When Dodge had finished reading the contents of the two pages, she shook out her arms like she was psyching herself up. "You aren't going to believe this. That night that Marcel told us about, where the town locked Willa up in the sensory deprivation box, this entry is from that night, *after* she got out of the box."

"My goodness," Birdie said, shrinking back.

"Right?" Dodge continued, tracking certain lines from the diary entry, running her fingers along them. "Here she says, *I knew when they returned and discovered the depths to which my passion ran, their blood would curdle where they stood and they would surely kill me. I have foreseen this night, and I will make it my own, not theirs. The ash that burns my tongue from the ninety-nine leaves of ninety-nine willows guides my vision and my path.* Apparently, she believed she could tie herself to the land and be reborn. Birdie, can you hold the flashlight for me? This part is especially disconcerting. I want to make sure you both hear it."

"Sure." Birdie pointed the light on the paragraph Dodge indicated.

"Okay, she writes, *The pedestals have been prepared according to their bond. With my blood, will be bound, and with my death, seal the ground. Through five I thrive, and ever after come alive.*" Dodge looked from Marcel to Birdie, her green eyes wide like a doe. "By five, does she mean..."

The creases between Marcel's eyes deepened and he gulped.

Birdie collapsed back against the bench. "*Us.* She means us."

Dodge frowned, slammed the diary shut, and handed it back to Birdie. "Well, good luck, lady. You're dead. And even if you're not, you're old as hell." She hurled her insults upwards at the mansion, then briefly quieted before addressing Birdie. "We can take her. Can't we?"

Birdie pressed her lips together in a thin line and shared a worried look with Marcel. He put his hand on hers and squeezed in solidarity.

"So what do we do now?" Dodge asked.

Eyeing the horizon, Birdie thought she detected the faintest hint of the coming sunrise. She sighed and stood up. "We're exhausted. Much as I don't like it, Adriana and Tom are not likely to want to get out of here at this hour. And I don't think any of us feel comfortable leaving them behind. Let's catch a couple of hours' rest and then pack up and get the heck out of here as soon as the morning hits."

Dodge and Marcel agreed. As they vacated the porch, Birdie stopped to go back and blow out the candles. She bent over the coffee table to do so. Then out of the corner of her eye, subtle movement startled her. Dodge and Marcel had already gone inside and without them, her adrenaline soared.

Birdie scooped up a candle, holding her breath to avoid accidentally blowing it out, and tiptoed over to a particularly crooked floorboard. A tree root pitched half the board up higher than Birdie had noticed any of the other times she'd been on the porch. She rubbed her eyes, the mistrust in her vision growing.

No further movement came from that direction. Birdie stood by the porch rails, facing out over the shrouded front roundabout and lawn. A fox screamed in the distance, further rattling her. The sooner they left this vile place, the better. Birdie extinguished the rest of the candles and went inside.

20

If Birdie had been a betting woman, she would've lost money on whether she'd be able to sleep after exploring the sinister art displays in Willa's room, followed by an encore of ominous admissions from Cromwell's diary on the porch. Her mind roiled at what they discovered, and still, she couldn't piece it all together in a way that made sense, besides the strong notion that they should all put as many miles of backwoods Georgia roads as possible between them and Willow Creek Mansion. Yet somehow, as soon as her head hit the pillow, Birdie fell into a dreamless sleep.

Consciousness returned like a flowing tide that lapped at the last thoughts she'd been mulling as she'd gone to sleep. Her muscles tensed. What time was it? The light didn't seem so bright through the curtains in her room. Maybe she'd only dozed off briefly. She pawed on her nightstand for her phone and cracked open her eyelids. The screen glowed, but she couldn't read any of the numbers. She squinted against the glare, and it reminded her of how an oncoming car's headlights flared like fuzzy stars in the night.

Birdie sat upright in her bed, drawing the covers up to her chin. Perhaps her eyes were dry despite the humidity. That sometimes lent itself to a slightly blurry awakening. She conceded that she likely wasn't well hydrated after yesterday. Fumbling for her purse, she withdrew a bottle of eyedrops and put them in. After blinking several times, the picture of the room around her cleared almost imperceptibly. Her jaw ached from how hard she'd been clenching her teeth. Her breaths came shallow and fast.

She tossed back the covers and hopped out of bed. Maybe it was only a matter of light. The room did seem so dark for the time of day it must be. On bare feet, she pattered over to the open window and shoved the curtains aside. The ripe sunlight of nearing midday flared, briefly blinding her, before bringing the forest and expansive grasses into sparse focus with a strangely white sheen. She still needed to squint to make out anything more than general shapes she could guess at, but it was better than when she'd first awoken.

Birdie let out an abrupt, harsh laugh, then covered her mouth at the sound. She'd been so full of hope for this residency, for the future of her photography career. And now...she rested her hands on the windowsill, and her fingers curled over an object whose feel she knew by heart, regardless of her eyesight—her camera.

She clutched it close, exploring every inch with her fingertips, her heart thumping in her chest when she reached the lens. The crack she'd inflicted on the poor instrument when she'd dropped it to save the dove was bad enough that she could follow its trajectory through the center of the lens like the way the red clay split in the water-starved ground. Her stomach fluttered with awful wings as she brought the camera up to her eye.

Her vision didn't seem as affected through the camera's perspective, despite the jagged cut in the lens that glimmered with rainbows when the sun caught it at the right angle. She scanned along the side lawn, which was a generous word given its state of disarray and overgrowth. The white sheen she'd noticed earlier hadn't been a trick of the sun or a side effect of her hindered vision. Instead it was a fine latticework of roots coating the grass, the base of tree trunks, traveling up the...

Birdie, camera still to her eye with one hand, for fear of losing the enhanced ability to see, slowly lowered her other along the windowsill where she'd found it. In her excitement earlier at having her camera, something she'd been missing like a phantom appendage, again close to her, she'd ignored a building dread. By feel alone, her trembling fingers reached for the mansion's siding and were met with the tickling of the root tips, slimy and newly born. From below, around the corner of the mansion, she heard off-key notes from Dodge's guitar float up from the porch, the strumming setting her teeth further on edge.

Like stampeding hooves, each element hammered her until she had a pounding headache and her pulse raced. Roots infested the grounds and threatened the mansion. Her camera—she'd never retrieved it from the Weeping Willow. How had it come to be on her windowsill? And Dodge—

Something bounced in the distance through her camera's lens. She zeroed in on it, skittish and uncertain she wanted to see anything else, worried her overloaded brain couldn't handle it. She trailed brown fur, a puffy white tail. Her shoulders relaxed. It was a simple rabbit. But then a creeping sensation tingled her nerves. The rabbit perched on hind legs, almost as if it were staring her down.

It had no ears.

A scream built in Birdie's throat. Before it escaped her lips, a smash of strings and a frustrated howl rang out from the porch.

Dodge.

21

Birdie again dropped her camera, not caring that it tumbled over the window ledge, and turned heel, sprinting for the door, down the stairs, and out onto the porch. Her skin prickled as she swore she felt the hundreds of eyes from Willa's portraits on her back, narrowed in fiery glee.

"Dodge?" Birdie skittered to a stop, the image before her stabbing her in the heart, the white-hot fire of witnessing a friend in agony.

Dodge lay crumpled in child's pose on the uneven porch boards, rocking slightly with her hands clamped over her ears. Her lips moved as she muttered something to herself. Spread like a halo before her were the splinters and shards of her beloved guitar.

"Dodge?" Birdie asked softly. She stepped around the broken guitar neck with mangled strings and kneeled by Dodge. Scanning around, she wondered why no one else came. Everyone in the house must've heard Dodge's screams. With Birdie's blurred vision, Dodge was a hazy outline of herself, her chestnut hair more than wild. Birdie was almost certain the woman shook with quiet sobs. Tentative, she touched Dodge's shoulder. "Hey, what's wrong?"

The musician yelped and shrunk away from Birdie.

"It's me. Talk to me. What's going on?" Birdie again reached for Dodge. The woman trembled in a way that threw Birdie off-kilter. She'd been scared by the recent occurrence at Willow Creek, more than she'd ever been in her life. But Dodge had been a sounding board, a voice of support and reason that helped her dig deeper in her well of strength than she'd thought possible. She *needed* Dodge to get through this. And if Dodge was breaking down—

When Dodge moved away from Birdie's touch for a third time, Birdie drew her in a tight hug. The musician first resisted, then quickly molded against Birdie, clinging to her. At last, she quieted. Dodge usually had something to say, anything, especially an ill-timed quip. Birdie lifted Dodge's chin and met her sad, green eyes. It was more than she could bear. "I'm here. What can I do?" Birdie asked.

Dodge tilted her head and knitted her brows. Tears welled. She lifted her hands to her ears. "I can't hear you."

"No..." Birdie sat back on her heels, slack-jawed. She felt temporarily out of body. How could she have missed it? All the signs were there, each of them had been affected. What she'd taken for Dodge's usual nonchalance had been her playing down losing her hearing. Birdie again hugged Dodge.

The rabbit with no ears, the birds with no eyes. Signs were everywhere if only Birdie could see them. She thought she'd been so aware, yet she had a sinking feeling she'd only gleaned what was on the surface. Pulling back, she raised her voice just below yelling. "Can you hear this?"

Dodge frowned but nodded. "Yeah, mostly."

"Okay," Birdie continued, getting to her feet. Then she helped Dodge up. "Let's go find the others. We're not staying here another night."

22

In the foyer, Birdie nearly tripped over several suitcases. Dodge righted her yet squeezed Birdie's arm with a look of concern. "How bad?" She gestured to Birdie's eyes.

"It comes and goes. I'm trying not to think about it." Birdie steadied herself on the banister and called upstairs. "Adriana! Marcel! Tom! Where are you?"

"Here." Adriana, somber and serious etched in the lines of her face, rolled a packed tote out of the kitchen and set it next to the luggage. "Marcel is finishing packing upstairs. Then we'll wake Tom and go."

Birdie opened her mouth.

Adriana held up a hand. "Sí, I know what I said. *Pero,* each of us appears to be unwell and at the very least, I think that rates a couple nights in a nice hotel and a visit to the doctor until we figure out what's going on. Don't you?"

Birdie imagined sinking into a puffy hotel pillow and drawing the plush comforter around her far, far from here. It sounded like heaven. She smiled. "I couldn't agree more."

Making what she hoped was her last ever trek

up the mansion stairs, past Willa's narcissistic notion of art, Birdie rounded up all their belongings, with Dodge close behind, and carted them down to the foyer in record time. Together with Marcel, they transported everything to the porch. Birdie stared at her car and bit her lip.

Dodge came up beside her. "You should ride with me. We can send someone back for it later."

"Thanks." Birdie wiped her face and tried not to laugh. Her camera, her car, her eyesight. What else did she have to lose that Willow Creek hadn't already taken from her?

Adriana popped her head through the door. "I'm going to go get Tom while you load up the cars. Be right back."

"Okay." Birdie turned to see Marcel backtracking up the porch steps he'd just been headed down, his keys in hand. "Marcel?"

She and Dodge pushed forward. Birdie had a queasy inkling she knew. The increasingly familiar white gleam blanketed the bottom step, the front drive, and the tires of their cars. She reeled.

"What is it?" Dodge asked.

"Roots," Birdie said, her voice loud enough for Dodge to hear.

"Roots?" Dodge shook her head, wringing her hands.

Marcel scribbled while they recovered from the realization. He shared it with them.

The words were a black smear on the paper to Birdie, and she frowned at them.

Dodge picked up on it and relayed his message. "He says, she's not going to let us go easily." Dodge's eyes widened as she finished. "She—you mean Willa Cromwell, don't you?"

Marcel gave a sarcastic curtsy and raised one eyebrow, as if to say, *Who else?*

The front door swung open, and Adriana emerged. A slight sweat beaded on her forehead, and her pulled-back hair frayed at her temples. "Is Tom out here with you?"

They glanced at each other. "No," Birdie answered, drawing the word out. "We thought you were getting him. Is he not in his room?"

"He's not in his room or the kitchen or the parlor nor anywhere else in the mansion that I checked." Adriana came out onto the porch and took Birdie to the side, lowering her voice. "I'm worried. There was blood on the bedsheets."

Birdie gulped. "Maybe he took his bandages off? But we should call the police. Or an ambulance."

Adriana crossed her arms. "I tried. The landline is dead. And you know our cell phones are useless out here."

Birdie clenched her teeth to keep from losing herself to a tirade of worry. Adriana looked about one strand away from snapping herself, and if Birdie freaked out, they might all devolve into shock. Birdie paced along the porch, away from the others. The sun dipped with late afternoon angles, and again she sensed a loss of time as it trickled away from her like the low water in the creek bed. They only had a couple of hours of light left if they were lucky. She refused to spend another night here. But she also wouldn't be able to live with herself, leaving Tom behind.

Gripping the porch railing, she heaved a big sigh. "All right, here's what we're going to do." Birdie pushed her shoulders back and feigned the assertiveness she wished she felt, hoping it didn't show to the other three. "Adriana and Marcel, you're going to do a lap around the immediate perimeter of the mansion and see if you see signs of Tom. Don't stray any farther than that, okay?"

The two nodded.

"Dodge and I will clear the tires and ready the cars. By the time you get back, we're going to jump in and go. If, for some reason, Dodge and I aren't here, you two take Marcel's car and leave. When you get to the closest town, have them send someone out here to help us. But do not, under *any* circumstances, come back yourselves."

Marcel shook his head.

Adriana stepped forward. "He's right. We're not leaving you."

Birdie quick-hugged them both. "Hopefully, you won't have to. But promise me, if we're not here, leave. Somebody needs to get out of here, somebody needs to get help."

Marcel squeezed her hand.

Adriana held her pinkie out. Birdie hooked it. "I promise, palomita."

Birdie and Dodge watched as they descended the porch steps and rounded the corner.

Dodge turned to her. "Should we find something to help us clear the tires?" She started toward the cars.

Birdie stopped her with an outstretched arm, pausing until she was reasonably certain the others were out of earshot. "We're not going to do that."

"What? But—"

"Look at those roots, Dodge." Birdie spread her arms wide, motioning to the sea of filaments. "This isn't natural. Willa Cromwell is doing this to us. Marcel's voice, Adriana's taste, Tom's touch, your hearing, my eyesight. Marcel is right; she isn't going to just let us leave."

"What are we going to do, then?" Dodge asked, her eyes wary, yet some of her former vigorous spirit returning.

"We're going to stop her."

23

After Birdie's announcement, she marched back into the mansion and then froze. In her gut, she knew it was the right move. In her heart, she overflowed to bursting with panic. In her head, she didn't have a clue how exactly she was going to stop a dead woman.

Dodge milled about, a coil ready to spring into action at the merest hint of a direction. She cast uneasy glances at Birdie now and again, probably unsure if she'd hear if Birdie said something and whether Birdie had any actual plan of attack. Though she knew Dodge wasn't pressuring her, Birdie still felt the heavy weight of figuring out what to do next.

She went over what they knew: Willa Cromwell brought them here fifty years after her suspected death. She'd been jealous of other artists' abilities that she didn't embody and had been unsuccessful at working through them to exact her vision. Obsessed with their five disciplines, Willa had created the creepy collection on display in her room: the cassette of her whispers, the abhorrent bowl of skin-shrouded peaches, the mystery box full of fingernails, the bone recorder, and the blood-red blindfold. Yet Birdie didn't think the answers to defeating the former lady of Willow Creek lay in that room. That was the shrine, the illustration of Willa's aspirations. It didn't speak to Birdie as the heart of the manifestation. Even if she knew what or where that was, how could she stop what was happening? Birdie hadn't seen anything resembling a ghost anywhere.

In the parlor, Dodge plopped into one of the wingback chairs next to the fireplace. Her movement rattled a couple of portraits on the wall behind her, including the framed photograph of the wretched Cromwell herself.

With my blood, will be bound...

Red blood bound the will. Red *paint* hidden on the frame's underside. Did it hold significance? It was a minor detail and perhaps a reach. In the time since arriving at Willow Creek Mansion, however, Birdie had become intimate with Willa Cromwell's nature. And someone like Willa, whose every move held horrific foresight and intention, wouldn't be so careless as to leave stray markings on the back of her portraits, would she?

Birdie darted around the couch and rushed to the photograph. As she snatched it off the wall, she locked eyes with Willa's shrewd image.

Mistake.

Her vision of the photo became clear as crystal while all else in the parlor surrounding it continued carrying the escalating, hazy film. Willa's forgettable frown morphed into a rictus grin, far too wide for her dull face. The movement revealed her imperfectly normal teeth and colored her overstretched cheeks with a dim, rosy hue. She beckoned Birdie to follow her gaze downward as her shoulders hunched and she ratcheted her body in jerking motions, as if battling the still nature of the photograph, to pluck an object out of frame from off the ground.

One hand cradled over the other, Willa obscured something that fought her tightening grip, something *alive*. In front of her malicious smile, she delivered up the creature to Birdie, unfurling stiff fingers with maddeningly slow theatrics to reveal a tiny, eyeless mourning dove—the *same* newborn dove Birdie had saved.

The barren-eyed baby bird cawed mournfully and pecked the framed glass. Birdie flinched. Willa leaned in close to its sparsely feathered head and screamed. The dove startled, flying at Birdie, its two starless voids coming for her. The bird's head smashed against the glass and cracked it, a starburst of webs searing outward from the point of impact.

Birdie's legs gave out from beneath her, and she collapsed to the floor, knocking the frame against the baseboard, shattering the glass before it clattered to the floor face up. With slow twitches and wreathed in shards, the photograph of Willa drew her arms toward herself and covered her eyes with her palms. The dreadful smile lingered as the movement ceased, the image again still.

Birdie's field of vision contracted, and she wailed. She wiped away the appalling phantom sensations of the dove's sticky down feathers fluttering against her throat, her chest. Fuzzy details drained away around her, so she was left with only the general silhouettes of objects. She wrapped her arms around her knees and breathed rapidly through her nose, catching a whiff of an earthy smell, odd for the parlor.

A lean shape stooped by her. Birdie reached out, touched Dodge's long hair, and gripped her shoulder. "Dodge, I—"

"I'm here." Dodge guided her to her feet, then bent briefly. Birdie assumed she now held the photograph, especially when she made a small sound of displeasure in her throat. "Is this her idea of a sick joke? Covering her ears like that—"

"Wait, she's covering her ears when you look at it?" Birdie asked.

"Yeah. Why? What did you see?" Glass tinkled as Dodge must've kicked it aside with her foot.

"Her eyes. She covered her eyes."

They stood close enough that Birdie felt Dodge's breath as she exhaled. "Forget her. Birdie, you came over here for a reason. I saw it on your face. What did you find?"

"It might be nothing. Flip over the frame." Birdie guided Dodge's hands to turn over the photograph. Blurred though it was, Birdie saw the red. "See this red streak of paint?"

"Yes. But what does that have to do with anything?"

Birdie licked her lips, quelling their trembling. "Nothing Willa has done seems incidental." She let go of Dodge's arm and went to the wall, then grabbed another depiction of Willa. "Ha! This portrait has one as well. It looks like it might be at a different angle."

"Here too." Dodge held up two more.

Anticipation welled in Birdie. "We're onto something. Let's gather up all the portraits in here. Push the furniture back against the walls and lay them out."

Together they cleared a large space on the rug. Dodge insisted on getting the portraits herself, but Birdie refused. While Dodge knocked down the higher up paintings in the foyer with a broom handle, Birdie maneuvered upstairs with the help of the railing. She'd wanted to double check Willa's bedroom for any additional ones.

Hands out in front of her, Birdie shuffled into the dark room and veered right toward the light switch. Her toe caught on a crooked floorboard, sending her careening into one of the display stands. The cloche toppled over and crashed to the floor.

"You alright up there?" Dodge called.

Birdie righted herself and patted her body. "Yeah, I'm okay." She navigated back to where the light switch ought to be, relief softening her tension as she flicked it on. The candelabra chandelier flooded the room with a warm glow accompanied by the sparkling constellation of glass that was once the cloche.

Hand over hand, she canvassed the walls and found the room contained no apparent portraits of the previous owner. On her way to the door to finish helping Dodge, Birdie paused by the broken glass. The red ribbon shimmered among the debris. She stooped and retrieved it. Letting it lay across her palms, she considered for the briefest moment putting it over her eyes. Then she remembered the effect the bone recorder had on Dodge and second guessed the prudence of that gesture.

Still, the blindfold was red as well as connected to her unique affliction, so she pocketed it next to the oracle deck card of the Woodcutter.

As she passed the uplifted floorboard, an amorphous flash of white against the wooden floors halted her. On bended knee, she got closer. The angle of the candelabra cast a shadow over the obstruction, and even with squinting, Birdie couldn't reproduce the white effect. Her blood ran cold as she reached her fingers into the break in floor. The stifled, humid air changed; it became cool and mineral. Like—

Clay.

A thousand tiny tendrils caressed her skin, searching, reaching, ensnaring. The roots grew with ferocity at contact with Birdie. She shrieked and jerked backward. A carpet of filaments vomited forth from between the floorboards and lurched toward her.

Birdie barreled toward the door, tumbled through, and threw the doors closed. She didn't wait. In an unsteady pitch, she raced down the stairs and met Dodge in the parlor. Out of breath, Birdie wrestled her unkempt hair from her face. "We're running out of time."

24

Dodge brushed the strands of hair out of Birdie's eyes, then squeezed her hand. "You're telling me, love. Thank goodness you can't see the baseboards. It's knocked them out like teeth, one giant rope of roots. It's also spread through the walls. Nearly every portrait I downed had some sort of growth clinging to it, not wanting to let it go."

Birdie shivered despite the pressing humidity in the parlor. Should they have spent this time clearing the cars of the roots? Perhaps they'd already be gone, far down the back roads, away from this vile place. She shook her head and moved over to the large collection of dusty portraits, blessedly face down on the rug in the middle of the room. The nape of her neck tingled at the idea of the roots infesting the walls and floorboards surrounding them. Luckily the red lines shone like reflective tape in the lamplight so that even she could see them.

She squinted at the curves and straight lines, the way they wound this way and that. "These must form some larger picture. Don't you think?"

Dodge squatted nearby. "Do you think these are part of a bigger drawing? Like a puzzle?"

Birdie winced. "Yes," she yelled. "Let's start piecing them together." How long did they have before Dodge could no longer hear her at all? As it was, Birdie's voice was growing raw trying to talk loud enough to be heard.

The two of them got to work. Anxiety bubbled up in Birdie the longer it took. "Dodge, I need that piece over there."

No response.

Shadows leaned at hard edges in the room. While the red paint was visible, everything else became light and dark sinuous blobs. Birdie moved around the couch to what she thought was Dodge crouched across the pile of portraits, but instead she discovered it to be an ottoman.

Birdie picked up the portrait she suspected was the crux to unlocking the entire image. Carefully traversing back to her spot, she discovered it was indeed the last of four portraits that lined up to form an oblong, enclosed shape with two pointed ends. Yet her relief at finding what was the equivalent of a corner piece on a jigsaw puzzle rested on a shaky foundation of worry. "Dodge? Where are you?"

A glint of silver flashed in the threshold. "Huh? Were you calling me?" Dodge's blurred figure approached. "Well, will you look at that."

"Where were you?" Birdie pressed her hand to her own chest and felt her heart thumping.

Dodge squeezed Birdie's shoulder. "Sorry. Didn't mean to worry you. I was getting this." The silver flashed again. "Oh, right. It's a knife. You know, just in case."

Birdie pursed her lips but simply nodded. It wasn't a terrible idea. She should've thought of it herself. But the knowledge that Dodge could see the state of the mansion and the threat, then felt compelled to get a knife left Birdie at the precipice of a quicksand of despair.

Dodge slapped Birdie on the shoulder, then bent near the coffee table to set the knife down with a clang. "We should be able to make quick work of this now that you've got an anchor section going."

In silence, they made steady progress. They'd finished all but the heart of the thing, the fanned arrangement eerily familiar, but Birdie wanted to see it in its completion before confirming. They were placing the last several portraits when—

Total darkness.

Birdie pawed at her eyes. "Dodge!" She shrank into the center of the framed monstrosities. Huddled in a ball on the floor, she clutched her knees to her chin. "Dodge?" Tears spilled down her cheeks, and her breath came so quickly that lightheadedness threatened to overcome her. How was she going to get through this if she couldn't see? It had come all at once, so suddenly. She might've steeled herself against a slow but persistent decline. Maybe. But the abruptness of it, the curtains of the world shut against her, possibly forever... It cemented her to the spot, inactive and unwilling to move.

As she sat there, a slight brush against her forearm made her jolt. "Who's there?" Something slick curled around her ankle. Birdie thrashed her legs against it.

The roots. They were coming for her.

Breathing through her nostrils, she calmed herself as much as she could manage, though her hands shook uncontrollably. She fumbled in her pocket and found what she searched for, making contact with the cool, smooth square of the phone against her palm. Birdie whimpered. She had a weak theory, but it had to be tested. It was all she had left. She had to try, right?

Again, roots hooked around her ankle and tightened. From memory, she frantically pressed the phone, issuing her command.

A cone of light spilled into the parlor. From the left, in the direction of the fireplace, a mat of white gleamed, connecting with Birdie's leg. Any joy over having some remaining vision, her theory confirmed that the power had gone instead of her eyesight, was sapped by terror. The light did nothing to tame the roots. They clamped like a vice as they crept up her calf, the tips digging into the fabric of her pants.

"Birdie!" Dodge leaped from the couch and landed next to Birdie. Metal winked as she slashed the roots.

The grip loosened on Birdie's leg as the roots retreated into the fireplace. Birdie rubbed her ankle, which had to be bruised at the least, then wrapped her arms around Dodge.

Dodge hugged her back fiercely. "Are you okay?"

Birdie nodded yet couldn't help a few tears that still gathered at the corners of her eyes.

"I couldn't hear you well enough in the dark to pinpoint where you were." Dodge wiped wetness from Birdie's cheeks and guided them to the couch. "Roots must've knocked the power out. We've got to finish this puzzle. *Now*."

Birdie gestured to the last of the portraits, scattered from the scuffle. Then she stood on the couch and shined the phone's light over the scene.

"Roger that." Still brandishing the knife in one hand, Dodge used the other to shift the final pieces into place. "All right, love. What're we looking at here? It better have amounted to something helpful, or I swear I'm going to hack and slash those darn roots away from one of the cars and get us the heck out of here."

All the red paint lines connected now to bring a new painting into being. Countless crimson leaves spread around a stout trunk. While it wasn't the most refined likeness, there was no mistaking it.

Dodge joined Birdie on the couch. "Heavens to Betsy. Is that what I think it is?"

Birdie cleared her throat. "The Weeping Willow." She handed the phone to Dodge before sitting back down on the couch, the knowledge weighing heavily on her heart. Her mind churned, connecting some loose threads and unable to resolve others. Sure, strange things had happened near the tree. It made sense that it had something to do with Willa. But what exactly?

Dodge settled in next to her, the tiny illumination creating a small sphere in which Birdie tried to imagine only they existed. Yet to push away the horrifying happenings around them was to deny the dire truth of their situation. Dodge put her arm around her, and Birdie leaned her head on her shoulder. Birdie had never had friends like this before. She wasn't about to let some envious, passion-obsessed ghost win, no matter how strong Willa seemed or difficult to find—let alone stop—she was.

"Do you think those roots are all the way from the tree?" Dodge asked.

Birdie sat up. Dodge had a point. Birdie had briefly looked up a couple of facts about willow trees before coming to Willow Creek. Now the information she'd casually shrugged at flooded back with sinister angles. She'd read that the roots of willow trees could travel three times as far as their height, which certainly made the mansion within the realm of the Weeping Willow's reach. They could also cause damage to structures, like cracking sidewalks or traveling through the plumbing in search of water.

Fifty years after my death...

Birdie rose to her feet, her blood running cold as she glared at the blood-red tree painted on the back of several dozen Willas. She turned so Dodge could see her mouth as she spoke. "Do you know what the lifespan of a weeping willow is?"

Brows furrowed, Dodge shook her head.

Birdie chewed her bottom lip and crossed her arms. Her heart thumped, and her muscles coiled in anticipation. She was on the cusp of something big. "Fifty years. It's fifty years."

25

"But we already knew the Weeping Willow had creepy vibes. That's not a surprise. How does this help us stop what's happening to us?" Dodge paced, the phone's light bobbing up and down, making the parlor's shadows jump.

"You're right." Birdie tucked her legs under her on the couch and tilted her head, half-expecting the tree painting to do something, anything, interesting. Dodge looked at her. Birdie cupped her hands, unsure it helped but didn't think it hurt. "I said, you're right."

"Darn tootin'." Dodge smirked and patted herself on the back with the hand that held that phone.

The movement set the fireplace aglow. Two coal-black eyes and a wide grin grimaced within a bone-white skull from the back of the firebox. Birdie yelped, burrowing farther into the velvet couch.

"What?" Dodge panned the light over the far side of the room, illuminating the coil of roots. "What did you see? Did it move?" She lifted the kitchen knife and pointed it at the fireplace. "Come back, you son of a gun, and you'll see just what I'm made of."

Birdie pried herself reluctantly from the cushions and placed a gentle hand on Dodge's wrist. "I don't think it moved. The light was playing tricks on my eyes." Pensive, she stalked the same route Dodge had earlier. "I've got an idea."

She relieved Dodge of the phone, then again stood on the couch. "Remember when I said ghost photography was baloney?"

Dodge grinned. "Yeah, you said it was baloney."

Birdie chuckled, hopeful butterflies fluttering in her stomach. She double clicked to open the camera app, held it high over the portraits, and snapped a quick succession of flashing photos, praying she got it all in the frame.

Dodge held Birdie's elbow to steady her as she hopped off the sofa. Birdie handed the woman her phone before stepping away to give Dodge space to look. She wrung her hands while waiting. "So? Was I right, or was I wrong?"

Silence as Dodge studied the photo. She swiped, swiped again, the brightness reflecting in her widened eyes. Then Dodge held the phone up and compared the images to the painted tree. "You were...right."

Peering over Dodge's shoulder, Birdie frowned. Six white spots glowed in the middle of the screen. She scrunched her nose. "Orbs?"

"What? No." Dodge pointed to each. "This is amazing. None of this shows up here on the actual painting. But look at these symbols." Dodge paused. "I'll describe them, though I think you might guess at five of the six. There's a mouth, a nose, a hand, an ear, and—"

"An eye." Birdie dropped her shoulders and sighed.

"Right. Here's where it gets interesting though. The last symbol is a skull. It's set right underneath the base of the tree."

"A skull?" Birdie glanced toward the fireplace. "Wait—underneath the tree—like in the roots?"

"Bingo." Dodge snapped her fingers. "That's not all. Each of the symbols representing, well, us, are connected to the skull via a squirmy line."

"Kind of like a root," Birdie said.

"Kind of like a root. Yes, ma'am."

Birdie led Dodge into the foyer, needing the space to think and talk away from the increasingly earth-scented parlor and shifty roots. She cast an unnerved eye at the floorboards. She may not know much about ghosts or witches or any of that. But they'd witnessed enough madness for a lifetime, and she felt grounded in her conclusion.

Ever since they arrived, since that day around the campfire when Marcel declared their creative intentions, the Weeping Willow heard. It connected them to Willa Cromwell, who siphoned their artistic predispositions, what she viewed as their innate talents.

Birdie massaged her temples before speaking the insanity aloud. "Willa has been below our feet this whole time. I think she's buried underneath the Weeping Willow. She *is* the Weeping Willow. We have to go to the tree. We have to figure out how to sever the connection."

"And if we don't?" Dodge asked.

Birdie reached for the doorknob to the front door. The way the roots hungered to wrap themselves around her body haunted her. "If we don't, then I don't think we'll make it to see the sun rise.

We'll be consumed in the fire of Willa Cromwell's passion."

26

At the top of the porch steps, Birdie and Dodge stood shoulder to shoulder. Pink rays of the setting sun dyed the land an ominous, sickly hue. The woods surrounding Willow Creek Mansion stirred restlessly in the advancing night. Ill at ease, Birdie detected no roaring hum of crickets nor speckled gold of fireflies. Humidity pressed its cocoon of damp heat against her face, her neck, her chest. Sweat gathered at her hairline. Even a deep breath to steady her nerves offered little reprieve, the air was so thick.

Birdie slipped her hand into Dodge's, who squeezed with reassurance as they descended. A sea of white carpeted the ground.

"Do you think it's okay to walk on?" Dodge halted them at the last step.

Birdie shrugged. Did they have much of a choice? "We're about to find out. Keep your knife handy," she hollered.

When her boot touched the latticework of willow roots, the soft give and squish of them made Birdie's skin crawl. She imagined them recoiling underneath her feet like millions of worms. Even

Dodge was quiet, which meant it also must've been particularly abhorrent to see.

Dodge tugged Birdie's arm. "Stop."

Birdie squinted. She couldn't see anything in the dying light. A span of white with dark objects speckled here and there. She guessed they faced the front drive. "What?" The skin on her arms prickled.

"All the cars are still here."

The news landed like a punch to Birdie's gut. She'd just assumed while they were inside, that Adriana and Marcel made the quick trip around the mansion and got the heck out of there. They should've been so long gone that help would be heading this way. But this meant help was not on the way. This meant that Tom, Adriana, and Marcel were missing. Where were they? What had Willa done to them?

Her blood curdled. She'd stupidly thought she had nothing left to lose. Heat simmered and bloomed from her chest up to her cheeks, spurring her to action. Birdie stomped farther down the trail, her memory of walking it every morning guiding her. Nothing was going to stop her from taking Willa down and getting her friends back.

"Wait!" Dodge called.

Everything in Birdie's being wanted to continue toward the accursed tree. But something in Dodge's plea cut through her rage. Just as Birdie stopped, her toe hit a root and she barely caught herself from falling. Her heart thumped wildly at how close she'd come to full body contact with the snaking mass of roots.

Dodge hugged her. "You're not in this alone, love."

Birdie sniffled, fighting tears. "I'm almost blind.

You're practically deaf. She has our friends. And we have nothing to fight her with." She wiped her nose. "How are we going to do this by ourselves?"

Dodge squeezed her close before releasing. "I'm only catching snippets of your words now, Birdie. But don't give up, okay?" She reached for something on the ground and pushed it into Birdie's hand. "You dropped this."

She ran her fingers over the glossy rectangle. The hope that blossomed that day when Dodge had read her cards seemed a mere wisp of itself. Yet she could imagine the cheerful lumberjack on the Woodcutter oracle card easily, as well as what Dodge had said to her. It meant a lot, more than Dodge likely realized. "*Vision or no, I have a feeling that you'll cut down any obstacle in the way of your dreams.*"

"We're going to figure this out." Dodge hooked arms with Birdie and started down the trail. "Together."

"The ring of keys." Birdie tapped Dodge's arm to get her attention. "The keys!"

"What?"

Birdie slowed. "We need the keys. If we can get into the shed, there are axes in there."

"Where are they?" Dodge asked.

Birdie took a second to remember where she'd put them. "Table. Foyer." She enunciated each word as loudly and clearly as possible.

"Okay." Dodge drew out the word, filled with hesitation.

"What is it?" Birdie put her hands palm up to indicate her question. She found herself speaking more and more through body language as best she could to make sure Dodge understood what she was trying to convey.

"I'm anxious to find the others, as I'm sure you are as well."

Birdie wished she could see Dodge's face. Until she couldn't rely on it anymore, she'd had no idea how much what someone said shown through their facial expressions. Yet Dodge held something back she didn't want to give voice to. Birdie waved her hand in circles, urging Dodge to finish what she was saying and get to the point. Her nerves rattled because she suspected what Dodge was going to say.

"I can move faster without having to guide you. To go back to the house, get the keys, then go to the shed to get the axes—that'll take quite a while. If I left you here, I could run." Dodge breathed shakily. "But I can't do that. You're defenseless out here." She touched Birdie's shoulder. "I can't lose you too."

Birdie closed her eyes, the difference in vision nearly imperceptible. She steeled herself and felt her way down Dodge's arms to the hard enamel of the kitchen knife's handle, then pried it out of Dodge's hand. She held it up to her chest with one hand and shooed Dodge away with the other.

"Are you sure?"

Birdie nodded, biting her lower lip to keep it from trembling.

Dodge hugged her again. Pulling away and holding Birdie's shoulders, she directed her until Birdie's back touched something firm. "Here. There's a tree trunk behind you, one of the harmless, dead ones, so you don't have to stand out in the open. I'll be back in a jiffy, and then we're going to take this old bag down for good."

Birdie admired Dodge's confident words and tried to hold onto them despite the worried tone that crept in as she'd said them. Footsteps carried Dodge away until Birdie could no longer hear them. Moist air attempted to warm her chilled bones, but to no avail. She gripped the knife so hard her fingers threatened to go numb. The ragged bark of the weakened tree behind her scratched her back through the fabric of her shirt. But she didn't care; at least it was something she could sense. Her eyes remained shut, pressed against the night, while her other senses came alive.

Her sense of smell amplified. Earth and wood, dirt and dankness surrounded her. She waited in the darkness, worried for Dodge, worried for her friends, worried for herself. In hindsight, she could easily chastise herself for not getting them out sooner, for not seeing all the signs. But how could they have known? Ghosts weren't supposed to be *real*. She'd much rather have had this all be a silly affair with Adriana admonishing them for their paranoia and superstitions. They could all be laughing over drinks right about now, with bright futures ahead, not the threat of death and who knows what else. Yet it was very real. Her breath was deafening in the expanding period of waiting.

An unexpected whiff of animal musk wafted from nearby. She stiffened.

She was not alone.

Birdie braced herself against the tree with her palm and brandished the knife in front of her, then held still. Something neared. She could hear the unsilence of it stalking in front of her. A bumpy dampness brushed her forearm, tickling her. Her skin crawled, imagining all sorts of heinous creatures it could be, and she did her best not to scream. Should she attack? Would it hurt her?

Bracing for the worst, she slowly opened her eyes. A slim, dark figure no taller than about midway up her calves about slunk around her legs. She could only see it because it stood out against the whiteness of the roots claiming the forest floor.

Birdie froze as the creature sniffed her shoes and legs. Judging by its size and the way it moved, it wasn't a dog. Then she thought about the screams they'd heard in the woods earlier in her stay. She bit her lip.

Foxes weren't exactly known to be friendly. They often bit people and carried rabies. Her grip on the knife tightened and she sorely hoped she wouldn't be forced to use it to defend herself. "Shoo. Go on. Get," she urged.

The fox whimpered and shrunk away from her but didn't leave. It remained out of reach and began to whine, a low keening sound that unsettled Birdie. Listening to the fear of this wild animal rivaled the torment of being alone. She wasn't sure how much more of it she could take.

The animal was terrified, just like she was. Under normal circumstances, she wouldn't even consider it. But normal circumstances flew out the window a couple days ago.

"I won't hurt you," she whispered and untethered her free hand from the tree bark. The animal inched toward her outstretched hand. Birdie breathed as steadily as she could but the sweat gathering on her palms betrayed her. She hoped she wasn't wrong. Fur and skull nudged itself into her palm. She gasped, relief flooding through her, running her fingers over its pointed ears and down its slick coat. It cowered but found solace in her touch. "Well, hello Mr. Fox."

Birdie kneeled, and the fox molded against her. Its warm body next to hers was a sorely needed comfort. She no longer felt adrift in a sea of terrifying blankness. The presence of the fox anchored her, calmed her. She had no idea how long Dodge had been gone. Time stretched in odd lengths at Willow Creek, but thankfully she didn't have to wait alone now.

The fox licked her cheek, and she smiled. She scratched it behind its ears and relished in the presence of a kindred spirit. Dodge should be back any second now. They just might make it through this thing.

Then the fox tensed. She hugged it around the neck, attempting to soothe it. "What's wrong?"

The fox thrashed its hind legs and whined.

Her hands traveled the fox's back to its legs. The fox screamed, startling Birdie back against the tree trunk, her knife knocked out of her hand.

It screamed and screamed and screamed, sounding like a woman being murdered. Birdie lunged forward and cried out in horror at what she discovered. The entire right leg was completely encased in twisted roots. She could feel them looping around, wrapping tighter and tighter until she heard—

Crack.

Icy terror seeped into her marrow. Birdie screamed in chorus with the fox until her throat went raw. She scrambled in search of the knife to save the fox. Her fingertips touched on the blade, and as she strained to grasp it, she found her feet wouldn't move, her efforts in vain.

A gnarl of roots cemented her boots to the spot.

27

The fox's fearful screams raised an octave, infused with unbridled pain. Birdie couldn't even unlace her boots to free herself, the roots operating like a python, working to swallow her whole. All the while, she stretched and strained to get the knife. If only she could reach it, if only she could save the fox, could save herself.

Silence descended. The fox stopped screaming.

Bile burned in the back of her throat. Roots encroached upon her calf. Tears clouded her eyes, not that it mattered. "Dodge..." she cried weakly. Birdie wept, forced to give up on her futile mission for the kitchen knife in order to avoid the roots that courted her wrists and declared their intent to claim her upper body in addition to her lower limbs. She cowered by the tree trunk, wanting to check on the fox, terrified to affirm its fate. "Dodge."

Thwack, thwack, thwack.

The hold on Birdie's boots loosened. The applewood smell of Dodge's hair wrapped around her as Birdie fell into the woman's arms.

"Oh my goodness, Birdie, are you okay?" Dodge cleared more roots off Birdie's legs. "It was near up to your knees. I got two axes from the shed, thank the Lord. Why didn't you use the knife?"

Birdie, recovering from her sobs, pointed to the fox.

"Oh dear." The swing of the axe zinged in the air again several times. "Okay, love, I freed him. He's not in good shape, though."

"He's alive?" Birdie rushed over. Dodge guided her hand until it met fur. Feeling around the fox's ribs, sure enough, it rose and fell with feeble breaths. She sunk into the rhythm, relief washing over her at the regularity of it. Maybe he would survive this. Birdie turned to Dodge next to her with a pleading look.

Dodge sighed. "Here, you carry the axes then." She grunted under the fox's weight as she lifted it in her arms. "Only 'cause the shed is across the way. We'll put him there and hope that's enough. If this is what's happening to the animals, we can't dillydally on our search for our friends."

Birdie nodded emphatically. While she carried the hefty axes and walked alongside Dodge, the huge white globe of the moon shone blurrily above. Clouds veiled its face, occluding it, or so she assumed. The moon being snuffed out was the last thing she saw as the remnants of any meager vision bled away completely. In the distance, more foxes screamed along with the shrieks of birds and other animals. She flinched as their agony echoed within her heart.

The shed door creaked shut. "Okay, your little buddy is as safe as he's gonna be right now. Let's go."

Birdie handed Dodge one of the axes while she kept the other. Not that she'd be much use with it, but it was better than nothing. They continued along the trail toward the campfire pit.

The deeper into the woods they went, the more every muscle in Birdie's body commanded her to turn heel and run. On the dense air rode the familiar smoky smell of the fire pit. In the undercurrent, she caught another scent, one that spoke to a primal part of her that said stay far, *far away*: ancient red clay churned unnaturally to the surface, a smell that signaled death and decay. A smell that should never be unearthed.

Her grip on Dodge's arm tightened.

Ahead, the cries of animals in the night crescendoed in a cacophony of pure torture. Birdie cradled her ears and prayed that Dodge couldn't hear it. When the sounds halted all at once, Birdie's rapid breaths echoed until she covered her mouth.

"What's happening?" Dodge leaned close.

Birdie couldn't decide which was worse: screaming or silence. She gulped and forced herself to listen. But it wasn't what she smelled, felt, or heard that scared her the most.

It was what she saw.

This wasn't any normal sight. She had no illusions that her eyes were somehow spontaneously healed. The woods around her remained shrouded in utter darkness. It was as if, now that her vision had ceased entirely, she was privy to a hidden view of the land, unveiled for her and her only. Crimson fireflies of light pulsed across the expanse of the forest floor as far as the eye could see. They winked in and out of existence, in and out, in and out, until each orb melted like puddles of molten metal and flowed into the veins of Georgia.

The cadaverously pale sheets of roots that infested the cracks and crevices of the property took on a blood-red glow, eerily reminiscent of the hidden painting on the back of Willa Cromwell's portraits. It collected at the extremities and streamed in a strange backward course toward the source of all their troubles, toward the destination that Birdie realized had always been calling to her, since the very day she arrived at Willow Creek Mansion—to the Weeping Willow.

28

Birdie locked arms with Dodge. She longed to talk to her, but even yelling now failed to get much across, and that seemed unwise anyhow as they neared the tree. The fluid-like surge of red light illuminated enough of the way that Birdie stumbled less on the silhouetted, bony knees and elbows of roots. She had her suspicions of what the red might be and got the distinct impression the essence flowed to feed the Weeping Willow. To what end?

Dodge slowed. "You ready?"

Ready for what? Birdie guessed Dodge meant to approach the trunk. Without knowing what lay ahead, having to completely depend on another person as her eyes, her heart banged like a drum and sweat gathered on her palms as she held onto the axe handle for dear life. Her other senses offered no additional information. Despite that, she trusted Dodge. They'd gone too far and too much was at stake to abandon post now. She started forward.

Dodge pulled her back gently. "Wait. Something's happening."

Innumerable leaves rustled in alarming contrast to the utter lack of a breeze. Branches groaned with movement. A curtain of darkness parted to reveal three blazing orbs, each a different shade of red—rose, blush, and rouge. Emotion welled in Birdie, taking her breath away and numbing her limbs. Her fear was a hollow pit that knew no bounds. She tugged on Dodge's arm.

"It can't be—" Dodge took two steps forward. "It's hard to see. We need to get closer."

They shuffled together toward the base of the Weeping Willow. Faint whispers tickled Birdie's ears and sounded like they came from the far right, the blush-colored orb. But Dodge inched them toward the rouge one, big and bright enough to make Birdie squint. Though she strained to listen, no sound emanated from it. The silence thickened and soured.

Dodge gasped. "No!" She pulled forward out of Birdie's grasp.

Birdie swayed, the sudden absence of Dodge daunting despite being able to hear her fret over whatever lay in front of them. Feeling her way with the toes of her boots, Birdie hit a solid object before she reached the orb. Dodge seemed to be circling around it without any real words attached to her pleas.

To hear Dodge losing her mettle petrified Birdie. Part of her wanted to find the woman and comfort her while also regaining her anchor in the brewing storm. Another part spoke to the urgency of the situation, to determining what blocked her path. Birdie bent over, her fingers searching for the obstacle. A solid sheath of roots, wide at the base, cascaded upward. She followed them around the trunk of the thing, up to waist height, then chest. Through an opening, the pads of her fingers landed on silkiness and fine ridges, a welcome respite from the oddly pulsating roots.

As she sought to determine what she felt, a familiar cologne broke through the overpowering smell of earth.

Marcel.

She shook with an echo of Dodge's panic and rose sharply. It was fabric she'd discovered, Marcel's embroidered vest. Heart to heart, the orb beat in time with her own stampeding rhythm. Birdie cupped his cheek and was met with a net of roots threaded across his lips. She dug her nails between them and his skin, but they were as one. To dislodge the roots meant irreparable harm to him.

Letting herself be flooded with memories of Marcel: his kindness, his desire for drama, his magnificent orations... That he should be silenced and contained, siphoned and stolen from, was unconscionable. Lava chased the icy terror from her veins, and she gathered it to her. She was going to need it.

Birdie pressed her forehead to Marcel's. "We're going to get you out of this."

She marched blindly toward the sounds of Dodge. After a hard hug and a shake, Birdie led her to the rouge orb in the middle. She knew what the three orbs were now, and she and Dodge had to think fast to get them out. Their lights were already much dimmer than they'd been when they entered the clearing.

The mustache and taller height told her the rouge orb was Tom. Though his hands were entwined in root encasements, his mouth was left free. "Birdie?" he croaked. "I can't feel. I think it should hurt, but I can't feel anything."

"Oh God, his lips are blue." Dodge held onto

Birdie, though her energy vibrated with a desire to pace.

Birdie nodded and repeated what she'd said to Marcel, quickly becoming a mantra she recited to herself in her mind. Maybe if she said it enough times, she'd believe it. She kissed Tom on the forehead and dragged Dodge to the final orb, blush waning like a wilting flower.

"Adriana," she called out. The dredges of her confidence expired as she assured her friend they were here to save them. Roots curled up the woman's nostrils and gathered at the corners of her mouth.

"I'm sorry," Adriana stuttered.

Birdie knitted her brows and stroked an exposed part of Adriana's hand. "What do you have to be sorry for?"

"I didn't believe. But they're real. They're very real."

Some of that frightening cold threatened to sap away the warmth Birdie stoked with her anger. "What is?"

"Ghosts." Adriana struggled to get the word out. "You shouldn't have come—"

Her last words were garbled, and Birdie touched the woman's lips and found her mouth wide open, her tongue shackled by roots. Adriana howled in agony, her speech muffled. Birdie wheeled backward.

Dodge caught her and lifted her up. "I can't hear them. But oh, Birdie, it's so awful to see them in so much pain. We have to do something *now*. I'm worried they're going to die."

Birdie placed her hands on Dodge's shoulders, then tapped her temple.

"Think?" Dodge shrugged away. "We don't have time to think. We brought the axes for a reason."

"No!" Birdie screamed. She'd explored the roots on their friends with an intimacy that Dodge hadn't and feared deeply what might happen if they were abruptly severed from their connection.

Dodge grunted, the head of the axe cut through the air with a metallic *whoosh* and landed in the densely packed roots with a *thomp.*

Hands pressed to her lips, Birdie cringed. She braced herself for the repeated sounds of Dodge attacking the roots, praying it would work, terrified it wouldn't. Instead, the ground trembled, followed by the smell of abysmal crevices yawning open. A sickening crack nearby was followed by the clay giving way. Birdie slipped and struggled to find her footing.

Air rushed by Birdie's head, and she ducked as something large darted by her toward Dodge. The musician yelped. Then awful gargling that could not —*must not*—be her friend emanated from that same direction.

The world tilted on its axis. Birdie scrambled toward the altercation. Frantic hands shoved her away, but Birdie fought them. A lumbering serpent of a root from the depths of her darkest nightmares had emerged and laced itself around Dodge's throat.

Her feet dangled wildly in the air. Birdie tried and failed to give her a reprieve. Dodge hunted for Birdie's hand, then clutched it. "Beatrice..." Scarlet radiance bloomed in her chest. "Go!"

29

Birdie cast her axe in a wide arc as she backed away from the basilisk of willow roots. "I'm not leaving you!" She hurtled her defiance at the Weeping Willow, knowing Dodge couldn't hear her but hoped that she knew she'd never abandon her. The revenge of plunging the axe into that wily root about her friend's neck was anticipatory sweetness on her tongue.

She shook her head and kept shuffling backward. As the scarlet orb slid toward the tree and joined the line of the three others, Birdie rightly predicted that Willa wasn't going to kill Dodge then and there. An open spot awaited in the semicircle as the orbs formed around the trunk of the tree. She jutted her jaw. "You want to add me to your collection?"

A root looped around her ankle, bringing her to the ground, knocking the back of her head hard against a coil of roots like they formed just for that malicious purpose. Stars burst across her field of vision, and for a moment, she was almost thankful for it. Then blackness crawled back in. Her hand was empty, her axe gone. The fleeting consideration to search for it recalled the way she'd looked in vain for the knife to save the fox.

"Fool me once," she muttered. The root tugged on her heel. Panic flared in her belly as she raced to untie her boot. Freeing her foot, she scurried, relying on her nose to lead the way. A rock sliced her heel, and she hissed, mingled with anguish and triumph. It meant she was close.

On hands and knees, she scoured the campfire pit. She raked over the cold coals, the charcoal grit coating her hands. By the pound of ash she sifted through, she'd found the center of the site and needed to widen her search. Swinging her arms back and forth in front of her, probing as fast as she could, a surge of excitement jolted her when she made contact with the tall plastic container, knocking it on its side.

Her elation dissipated almost as quickly when she heard a *glug, glug, glug*. Wetness soaked the ground, and a foul chemical smell choked her lungs. Stifling a cough, she cursed and righted the lighter fluid. She shook the container, only to be answered by the faintest sloshing within. It wasn't enough.

A vice clamped around her calves. Birdie scraped the clay in her immediate vicinity and, a second before she was lifted into the air by her heels, enclosed her fist around the tiny metal case.

The lighter.

The root whipped her higher, and she swung like a pendulum, dizzy with the blood rushing to her head and sick to her stomach. Still, she clung onto the last hope she had.

When she'd stopped swinging, a light wind caressed the nape of her neck. It carried with it a rotting stench and noxious whispers—whispers she'd heard before near the Weeping Willow. This time, the words were clear and strong. "*With your essence, talent be found, and with my passion, willow be crowned. Through five, I thrive, and ever after come alive.*"

Birdie sneered and spit at the roots. If this was the end, she wasn't going to keep her mouth shut. She'd been doing that her whole life. "Enough theatrics. You can't really think that you'll be a good artist by stealing our abilities? That's not how it works."

The breeze died. Quiet cycloned around her, drowning Birdie in darkness and desolation. Birdie sensed only the putrid, crushing extensions of Willa. Birdie couldn't even see the ebbing orbs of her friends. Out of the absence of light, the dagger of a root lashed her cheek. The wound stung, and hot blood dripped into her eyes.

Air whirled around her in an enraged frenzy. "*You lecture me on artistry? You, who strives to reveal the truth of the world through lenses yet are afraid to truly see?*"

The truth in Willa's question burrowed inside Birdie's aching heart. She'd been pretending to reach for what she'd wanted so long, but deep down, hadn't she sabotaged everything that could've been fruitful, that could've realized her vision? And out of what—fear?

A python of roots enveloped the lower half of her body. The more they consumed her, the further she felt from herself. Lightheadedness drew over her like a fuzzy blanket, dreadful in the ease with which she could succumb. Ruby bloomed in her chest, a flower of potential that had long lain stymied under her direction but which seemed poised to blossom beyond her wildest dreams under Willa's guidance.

Harsh chuckles buffeted Birdie's ears. "*Pathetic.*"

30

Willa writhed over Birdie's ribs, her neck, then wreathed across her temples and spread a sheath over her eyes. Pressure built against her eyelids as threads penetrated her lashes. Filaments wriggled over the sensitive flesh of her corneas.

Birdie screamed.

The sound rang raw and hollow, mournful and agonizing. Alone. Her world was black and ruby as Willa dragged her to her place among the others. The movement jarred Birdie out of her shock and brought her attention to the cool metal, held so tight in her palm that it surely left a mark.

Drawing into herself, Birdie imagined that what was happening to her, to her eyes, was instead happening to someone else. She concentrated on her hands and carefully opened the lighter. With smooth motions, she flicked it and waited to feel heat.

Nothing.

She needed to act fast before they reached the semicircle. Birdie flicked again. Then again. Like a long-fingered hand, roots shot out and encased her wrist. Birdie whined as they wrenched so tight they cut off her circulation. Her fingertips grew numb.

"I admire your tenacity. However futile. You cannot save your friends. You cannot save yourself."

Birdie's nostrils flared, and she howled. She gave the lighter one final flick.

Heat exploded into life; the skin on her fingers and palms seared with it. The wetness on the ground, the lighter fluid, it was all over her hands.

Her hands were on fire.

The roots loosened their handcuffs and distanced themselves from the flames. While Birdie's angry howl distorted into shrieking, Willa laughed and laughed, a maddening sound like the rattling of dry bark.

Wild and furious, Birdie splayed her fingers in claws and plunged them into the thick of Willa's roots. Freed, the fire left her and hungrily spread over the exposed roots.

Gusts of wind bellowed in the night. Burnt embers pillowed the air and stung Birdie's skin. Stifling smoke filled her lungs. Willa's grip on her, suspending her in a precarious state, slackened and released. Birdie fell an untold number of feet to the hard clay below, bruising her arm and shoulder with her impact.

Proliferating patches of fire surrounded her; a deafening crackling roared in her ears. She cradled her hands and curled away from the boiling heat.

What had she done?

31

Branches snapped thunderously and quaked the ground with their fall from the Weeping Willow's canopy. Birdie cowered, withdrawing from the flaring heat and sensing the chaos around her. The fire must've traveled from the roots back to the tree. She might've smiled at the imagined picture in her mind of what the great tree looked like aflame, its thousands of thick leaves combusting the evil within. If not for the imminent threat of being burned alive, let alone what was happening to her friends, she would have.

Her hair slick with sweat, her tongue parched, Birdie burrowed herself in her spot. Anxiety burbled over as fire closed in. She tested all directions but couldn't locate a way out. What if she ran, just picked a point and went for it? Every time she crouched on the balls of her feet, ready to do or die —likely die—she couldn't muster enough courage. The echo of the fire on her injured hands warned her away from any action that would result in that feeling over her entire body.

A branch splintered directly overhead. Though

she looked up, Birdie met only darkness. She recoiled and braced for impact.

Someone hooked their hands under her arms and hauled her several feet out of the way. An enormous smash behind them signaled how close she'd come.

"Are you okay?"

Deep voice, rough hands, strong and tall. "Tom!" Birdie threw her arms around and
bear-hugged him.

"Oh thank goodness, palomita. We were worried." Adriana joined the hug.

Birdie drew back, her heart thumping nervously. "Dodge?"

"I'm here." Dodge slipped her hands around Birdie's shoulders and kissed her on the cheek. "Marcel is here too. We're all okay. Thanks to you."

"Come. Let's get closer to the creek and away from the fire," Tom said.

Dodge led Birdie, moving at a good clip. Fresh air was glorious against her skin. Birdie inhaled and exhaled with gusto, happy for the oxygen. The ground changed texture under her bare foot, and she stepped onto the gravelly sand. "Ow."

"What?" Adriana asked with concern. Dodge didn't slow her pace.

"Lost my shoe and cut my foot. It's okay. Let's keep going. I burned my hands badly, though." Birdie's toes met refreshing water, a few inches deep.

The creek. They were free.

"Hopefully we can get you—get us all—to a hospital soon." Adriana gently lifted Birdie's forearms, turning them over. "Ay, díos mio, they aren't pretty."

Perhaps one of the few times since her vision went, Birdie was relieved she couldn't see. She wasn't sure she could stomach what the damage looked like based on how it felt. She tried to tell herself that wounds often feel worse than they actually are, but Adriana wasn't helping.

Wait.

Why hadn't her vision returned? Her stomach flip-flopped as if in freefall. But the rollercoaster was supposed to be over.

"Adriana, can you tell me what's happening? Is the tree destroyed?"

The woman sucked in a breath. "It's completely engulfed." She spat. "Good riddance."

Birdie relaxed her shoulders and stood silently for several moments. Ashes rained down in great fluffy heaps, tickling her arms and nose. When she breathed, she couldn't help but take in some of the floating soot. It made her think of Willa, eating the ash of ninety-nine leaves of ninety-nine willows, thinking it gave her some kind of foresight. She guessed it did.

As Birdie mused, awaiting the return of her vision, a lump congealed in her throat. She'd assumed that if they defeated Willa, they'd all get their senses back. What if they were gone for good? A tidal wave of terror washed over her.

Then it came.

First, in one crisp drop on her forehead. Then another on her cheek, another on her lips, another, another, another.

Rain.

The heavens pummeled them with a deluge of water, the long-held breath of drought exhaled upon them in a sweeping bouquet of mineral scents and cool liquid. Birdie gasped at the excruciating relief of it against her burned skin. The others around her at first made exclamations of joy, but among the rising sizzling of extinguished fire, their cries turned to anguish.

Birdie gripped Dodge's arm, who'd grown stiff as a board. "What's happening?"

No response. From her left, Tom groaned in despair. To her right, Adriana recited vehement prayers in Spanish. The rain passed, leaving a muted, otherworldly atmosphere in its wake—no crackling branches, no roaring fire, and no static of dying flames.

Cold sweat gathered at the nape of Birdie's neck and her lower back. Her clothes soaked, she shivered in a sweeping frigid air that swirled around them with no discernible direction from which it arrived. The muddy ground shifted underneath their feet, a rolling wave of soil that gave them no option but to be drawn back to what was left of the tree. Birdie didn't need to see it, she knew it in her bones as if she were a magnet of an opposing polarity, unable to break free from the attraction.

Adriana screamed, Tom cried, and Dodge locked arms with Birdie like a vice as they rode on the crest. Birdie assumed Marcel was with Adriana, though there was no way to be sure as he still made no sound.

An ethereal glow pulsed in the red-rooted network of veins toward a source just beneath their feet. It poured into it and poured and poured until the cup overflowed and spilled violently over, exploding in a supernova of essence.

Birdie covered her eyes in the blinding blast. Darkness again blanketed her vision. Tremors shook the land and giant vipers of roots slithered in the clay, knocking Birdie and Dodge to the rain-drenched ground. In front of them, with an ear-splitting tear, a fissure ruptured the earth.

"Hells bells." Dodge's voiced dripped with fear. "The clay, the roots, the *bones*."

Birdie huddled close with Dodge, her imagination conjuring up the worst. Adrenaline coursed through her, and though her lips trembled, she remained still as stone. When she couldn't take it anymore, she called out. "Adriana, for the love of all that's holy, please tell me what's happening."

Adriana halted her incessant prayers. "It's horrible—" Her voice cracked. "It's just standing there, staring at us. *Esqueleto rojo*."

Seconds of silence stretched an eternity. Birdie didn't recognize the phrase, her Spanish far too rusty and panic clouding her ability to think. Even when she guessed at its meaning, there was no way it could be that. Yet they'd known Willa was buried beneath the Weeping Willow.

Birdie bit her lip so hard she tasted sweet iron. The limbo of waiting, not knowing, not acting, crowded in on her, stealing her breath. Then her mind flooded with a snapshot so pure that she felt she'd been dunked into an ice bath.

Shivers traveled up her spine as she pictured what approached: the reanimated bones of Willa Cromwell, packed and caked with slick, red Georgian clay that oozed from between her jagged ribs; a skeleton intertwined with roots so numerous they congealed like a million worms, coiling around the muck-slathered humerus and femur bones like slithering muscles; a vicious cadaver lurching toward them with glowing red eye sockets and a crooked grin, hell bent on their destruction.

In the quiet traveled an awful, bone-chilling

creak. The creature that was Willa Cromwell, *esqueleto rojo*, unhinged its jaws and let loose a soul-shattering shriek.

Birdie cradled her ears. The smell of earth and death left Birdie choking. A torrential current of terror beyond any she had ever known overwhelmed her system.

Crack. Crack. Crack.

Like stiff joints cracking that hadn't moved in ages, it came slowly and picked up speed with each petrifying step. The ground thundered with the force of it. Soon it would be right on top of them.

"No, no, no." Adriana repeated the plea over and over. "It's coming for us—*run*!"

32

Birdie dragged Dodge to her feet. When she didn't budge, her shoulders planted toward the coming abomination, Birdie slapped her cheek lightly. She hated to do it, but she didn't see what choice she had.

It worked. Dodge came to life, and together they ran.

They sprinted. Running blindly, trusting Dodge's lead, they got farther than she dared hope. For a brief flash, she believed they would make it. Grit stung her naked heel, and Dodge's grip on her hand bruised burned tissue, yet Birdie used the pain to fuel herself faster and faster, pumping her legs, trying to keep up with Dodge's pace.

Frenzied screams erupted in the chaos as they scattered, so high pitched and akin to a frightened animal that Birdie couldn't tell which of her friends unleashed the sound. Had Willa gotten them? What would she do to them if she caught them now? Birdie didn't think their benefactress had a benevolent bone in her body. Willa was on the warpath, and there was no telling what horrors her twisted mind had in store for them.

Birdie slipped.

Mired in mud, she scrambled to find purchase, to regain her footing, but it was fruitless. She swam in a blind sea of dirt and fear, adrift and alone. Dodge had disappeared, or at least, Birdie couldn't find her. She conjured all sorts of monstrosities just at her heel, about to swallow her whole.

Birdie reached and finally clasped Dodge's hand. "Oh, thank goodness," Birdie sighed as she came to her feet.

Then, the fingers lengthened, and the palm disintegrated. It hadn't been Dodge at all, but instead a cruel prank designed to lift her heart and then shatter it. She flinched, expecting Willa's roots to wrap around her body and squeeze until she was no more. That would've been a mercy compared to what Willa had in store for her.

Untethered, Birdie stood, swaying, unsure if she should run. The roots left her in peace, and that was somehow worse. She hugged herself, and frustrated tears gathered at the corners of her eyes.

Birdie jumped—a piercing shriek ahead. Was that Dodge?

She dared step forward, and a blinding white flash blazed too bright against her unadjusted eyes. Throwing up her arm as a shield, she moved in another direction only to wince at the same effect.

Flash. Flash. Flash.

From every side, from above, they compelled her to seek refuge in the mud, making Birdie withdraw into as small a ball as possible on the ground. Her retinas ached, and her nerves were on a razor's edge. The air became hot and close, choking her with its proximity.

The violent flashes ceased at last. Something

was so familiar about them. When the harassing light eased, it dawned on her: they were camera flashes. Dread flooded her system, and she tried to get to her feet only to hit her head on a hard ceiling not a few inches above.

The movement threw her back down. She instinctively rubbed the knot forming on her scalp and shook off what she could of the bewildering haze it induced. Birdie lashed out, scouring every crevice of her container. Her anguished screams reverberated back at her and mocked the futility of her desire to escape.

Birdie was trapped in the sensory deprivation box.

Being confined a second time did nothing to alleviate her panic. Oxygen became a concern as she hyperventilated. Cloying sweetness coated her throat and displaced whatever was left of the good air out of her lungs. She snapped her mouth shut and focused on steady breaths through her nostrils.

Again, familiarity rattled her. She knew this smell. It was Adriana's peach cobbler, only amplified to an abrasive degree, as if she was inside the oven as it baked.

Before she had time to think, Marcel's voice, lilting and sure, floated through the crushing darkness. She felt as if years had passed since she'd heard it, and she couldn't help but feel a tiny amount of relief. But then she heard his words.

"Witness, o tree of willow weeping,
We impassioned five seek our reaping.
Seer, singer, speaker, sculptor, server,"

As Marcel spoke the incantation, his voice distorted and transformed, becoming the bland, ominous voice of Willa Cromwell.

"Bestow upon me the fruit of my fervor.
Willow, my body planted you revive,
Imbue my bones with their essence, alive."

Searing pain erupted at Birdie's fingertips. Insidious roots pried underneath her nails and sought to loosen them from her tender flesh. Birdie whined and retracted her hands, hugging them against her body while tiny tendrils darted and pressed themselves to her arms, her chest, searching, searching.

Dulcet tones emanated with no clear source. The box heaved inward upon her shoulders, her back, her toes. It depressed so low that she had to twist her head toward her knees as it leaned on her upper spine. A background melody of Dodge's guitar strums, played to a grisly perfection Birdie had never witnessed, offered no solace. Instead it brought a further grimace and a sickness in her heart. Would she be crushed to the warped soundtrack of her friend?

She lost more space for her footing and tucked her feet back as far as her joints would allow. Her toes came in contact with something smooth and cool. Birdie contorted herself and managed to take the small rectangle in her hands. It was no bigger than a business card and as she ran her fingers over it, she detected the etched writing that allowed her to recognize it for what it was: the brass-plated warning.

"Take from the Weeping Willow, and the Weeping Willow will take from you."

Birdie laugh-cried, a hoarse, sad sound. "All this

over a photograph I took?" She quieted. The photograph must've connected her to the tree and allowed Willa to steal her sight. They'd each been bated into taking an element of the Weeping Willow by the sheer nature of the grant itself. Willa's brilliant design. Yet, Birdie *had* given the tree a secret. Had that been why she'd been able to perceive other things about Willa that the others hadn't? What if she gave more?

"You want my talent so bad?" Birdie dug into her pocket and retrieved the silky red blindfold. "Here. Take it. I give it to you freely. Let's see if you're as good as you think you are, *Willa.*"

33

Hastily, Birdie looped the blindfold over her eyes and tied it at the back of her head, ignoring the unpleasant snag of tangled hair she caught in the process. She wasn't exactly sure what she expected to happen. Everything affecting her in the sensory deprivation box harkened back to the accursed objects in Willa's collection, kept on presentation in her room. Dodge had a strange interaction with the bone recorder that represented her own unique ability. The blindfold had an equally odd magnetism for Birdie. Yet there was no way to know the effect it would have, if any.

It was a guess, a bluff, a chance.

Birdie waited. Her muscles ached with exhaustion and cried out for more room. Her emotions resided in a place beyond fear, beyond hope. She was trapped with no way out at the whim and mercy of a vile, cold-hearted ghost. A well within her rose and overflowed with a steel liquid. It flowed through her veins and filled her with a resolve that contrasted the dire situation.

She felt nothing. Birdie cupped her hands over the blindfold and depressed it against her lids.

That's when she noticed the silent stillness: the guitar no longer strummed, the roots no longer sought to dismantle her, the smell of earth and blood returned. Her eyes tingled with a newness she couldn't place. Dizziness, like being perched at the edge of a cliff, swam in her head.

Birdie opened her eyes.

She was free from the knitted box of roots. The world was awash in a crimson hue and outlined in blood-red fireflies wherever life grew or roamed. Her view panned to the left, despite her head remaining immobile. A sensation not far from car sickness bubbled inside her. What was happening?

Before her, four orbs pulsed: rose, blush, rouge, scarlet. She blinked, and the vision remained as if she had not. Birdie couldn't look away. Indeed, the lights appeared to move toward her. Or she to them? Disoriented, she forced herself to identify her friends. Muddy, wet, and bloody, Tom held Adriana; Marcel huddled together with Dodge. So much time had passed since she'd been able to see them clearly. The terror in each of their expressions was too much to bear.

Skeletal arms infused with roots raised in front of Birdie as if they were her own and lunged toward her friends.

Birdie screamed.

She reeled as the attack halted and the surrounding forest whipped by until she zeroed in on a small figure in the distance. Birdie planted her feet in the ground and knew she did not walk toward it, yet her eyes disobeyed. As she drew closer, Birdie saw the intended target—*herself*.

Birdie's vision hadn't returned. She saw the world through Willa Cromwell's eyes.

Surprise hummed through her, and she sensed an echo of it in the ghost, that Willa had never intended for her instruments to be used against her. Willa overcame the jarring turn of events faster, and the distance between them closed. Birdie's indifferent calm quickly washed away, replaced by a tight string of anxiety, the dawn of another day slipping through her fingers.

The blindfold in tandem with her offering allowed her to borrow Willa's vision. What was she going to do with it? Birdie clenched her jaw and teetered to her feet. While her eyes lied and said she raced forward, her body insisted she stood still. Bile rose in her throat.

"No," she whispered. She wasn't going to let another opportunity pass by. Birdie leaned into the sensation and used Willa's eyes as if they were her own. A trickling channel between them opened like floodgates. Passion surged hot as fire through Birdie, and she made herself a lens in which to focus it.

Willa was nearly on top of her. Birdie hardly recognized herself. It wasn't that she was caked in red clay or looked like she'd been through hell and back. It was that she stood tall and strong, sure and confident, in a way she'd never seen reflected in herself before.

A glint of metal flashed nearby her own body as Willa closed the distance between them. Birdie watched herself, felt herself, catalyze into action, the mirror image in Willa's eyes the key to dropping to a bent knee, swiping up the axe handle, and positioning herself to strike.

"I am the Woodcutter." Birdie plunged the head of the axe deep into Willa's shoulder.

34

The axe sunk into the fleshy roots and hit bone with a sickening crunch. Willa bellowed with sonic fury and thrashed against the instrument. Locked in battle, Birdie held onto the handle, unyielding, despite the searing agony coursing through her burned hands. The struggle loosened the socket and dislodged Willa's arm. Dangling by a weak root thread, the dismembered limb tumbled to the ground.

Triumph filled Birdie's face as she cast the axe back for another blow. Then came swift retribution —Willa hit her across the stomach with the broadside of her other arm. The wind knocked out of her, Birdie skidded several feet away and curled into a ball, gasping. Her axe skittered just out of her reach. She struggled to overcome the blooming pain that throbbed in her abdomen.

With horror, Birdie witnessed Willa unleash cascading roots toward her discarded arm. They wrapped around it, lifted, and wrenched the bone back into its rightful place. The root-infused ghostly skeleton flexed its arms, as if for Birdie's benefit, and laughed dryly.

Again Willa advanced upon Birdie.

Birdie pushed up and slipped, holding her torso. She choked on a sob filled with anguish and exhaustion. Willa laughed louder until it became the very air Birdie breathed, seeped into her skin, cemented her to the dirt. Birdie strained to reach the axe, her fingers barely clasping the handle once more.

But it was too late.

Willa extended awful, bony talons, conductors obeying the roots curled around their digits, and scooped Birdie up, high above her skull. Birdie managed to cling to the axe, drag it with her, yet it was useless in her hands.

Cocking back, Willa threw Birdie against the trunk of the Weeping Willow. Stars should've burst in her view from the force of it, but as she fell in a heap at the base, all she saw was the steady gaze upon her own limp body.

Birdie lay still.

Deep aches coated her back. She wasn't entirely sure nothing was broken.

"Birdie!" Dodge screamed. "Get away from her, Willa, or so help me, I'll rock your world so hard you'll wish you were never born!"

Birdie's world careened with retch-inducing speed as Willa spun around to face those who dared confront her: Dodge, braced with her own axe, stood hurt yet defiant, green eyes furious, with Adriana, Marcel, and Tom at her back.

"No..." Birdie cried weakly, lifting her hand toward them. Each of her friends was willing to fight for her, for themselves. Despair curled itself around her like a snake. Each of them was going to die in the process. Willa could regenerate. How could they stand a chance against her?

Willa's haunting laugh mocked her and held terrible promises that flooded her with dread.

There was no time left.

The vision of Dodge recalled the Woodcutter card. But Birdie had tried that and failed. It was just a stupid card anyway. Why did she think it meant anything more than that?

Pink sunlight winked over the horizon. With Willa facing away from her, Birdie couldn't use her vision to guide her own movements. The only thing she could feel was the stout tree trunk behind her.

The trunk.

On hands and knees, Birdie forced herself up. She swallowed a scream as her injuries bade her to surrender. Willa was seconds from Dodge, who held the axe bravely, and the others.

It wouldn't be enough.

Birdie scrambled and blindly searched the area around her. She found what she was looking for. On unsteady feet, she touched the bark and positioned herself as best she could. Her head spun from exhaustion and sheer physical trauma. Bile threatened to double her over. She took several sharp inhales through her nose, steeling every last bit of herself. Willa wasn't going to take her friends from her without paying the ultimate price.

Birdie arched her back, swung with every ounce she had left, and plunged the blade of the axe into the Weeping Willow.

The scream from Willa was different: agonizing, scared. Birdie's screams echoed in time with the monstrosity. This time, Birdie didn't take a moment for victory. Instead, as Willa abandoned the attack on her friends and came for her, Birdie hacked and hacked at the trunk.

With each swing, Willa slowed and weakened. Birdie watched herself through Willa's eyes as she swung rhythmically to rend yawning gashes into the bark. The tear-stained crimson blindfold shimmered in the birthing beams of sunlight. Birdie's arms appeared strong and legs steady, despite the excruciating stinging in her bare heel. Each swing cost Birdie precious tissue on her palms, yet her grip remained as she howled until she was hoarse and attacked the tree with relentless fury.

Before Willa reached Birdie, she stumbled to her knees. Her wooded talons extended towards Birdie's leg, very nearly touching her skin. *"I would've amazed the world. I would've—"*

Birdie drove the blade to bite deep into the flesh of the tree.

Willa collapsed. The roots slithered away and withdrew from her clay-encrusted bones. It was the last thing Birdie saw before she was again drawn into darkness. She rested the head of the axe at her side as spent adrenaline and her exertions caught up with her.

Adriana relieved Birdie of her axe. "Let me help, palomita."

Dodge, Adriana, and Marcel took turns chopping the wide trunk. Some of them cried as they did it, some yelled, some both.

"Stand back," Tom instructed as they neared the end of their work. From the strained crease at the corners of his eyes, Birdie knew it had been difficult for him to stand by, all that strength in those muscled arms and just as much anger at Willa as any of the others, if not more. But Adriana had insisted he not aggravate his bandaged hands.

With the trunk now severely weakened, Tom stood tall, squarely faced the tree, and sent a powerful kick against the butchered bark. Birdie looped her arm within Dodge's and listened to the satisfying groan of the Weeping Willow as it toppled over, splashing into the creek, branches splintering. The artists collectively gasped, the veil of its power at last retreating and lifting its burden.

Oranges and pinks pierced the sky in magnificent splendor. Overcome by joy, Birdie wiped tears from her cheeks, hardly able to believe the sight before her. She turned to Dodge and smiled. "It's beautiful."

"That it is, love." The light warmed Dodge's chestnut hair and illuminated a tired but radiant smile in return.

"You can hear me?" Birdie squeezed Dodge in a crushing hug.

"Ow. Easy does it, lumberjack."

They both chuckled and nursed their wounds.

"It's so good to hear you laugh, little bird of Georgia."

"Marcel!" Birdie didn't care how much it hurt; she hugged him too. She gave equally big hugs to Adriana and Tom.

Marcel eyed the pile of Willa Cromwell's bones warily and kicked them with the toe of his shoe. "Good riddance." The femur rolled off the pile toward him and he jumped, sending them into another fit of laughter, weary yet mirthful.

"Come on, let's get out of here," Birdie said. The

five of them formed a procession on the trail, faces warmed by the rising sun, the felled Weeping Willow at their backs.

35

The gentle chirps of crickets in the front yard soothed Birdie. Golden sunlight filtered onto the porch in slivered streams as she sipped her honeyed sweet tea, the cool liquid bringing back memories of summers at home. After they'd returned to the mansion, their hunger got the best of them, and they agreed to Adriana's offer to cook them up a big brunch before they got on the road. Birdie managed to get a call out to a local wildlife rescue group, who'd instructed her on how to dress the fox's wounds and promised to come out the next day to check on him.

With the wide-cast nets of white roots disappearing as if they'd never entangled the forest floor nor prevented their leaving, the group saw no reason to make the long drive out of Willow Creek until they were at least rested and recovered. Especially after bellies full of good food, several rounds of drinks, and many bouts of relieved jokes and recountings of their near brush with death, Tom, Adriana, and Marcel fell prey to their own eyelids that early afternoon.

Before Birdie and Dodge succumbed to much-needed slumber, they sat together on the couch in the quiet hush of the parlor. After their brunch, they'd all cleared the room of the clutter of portraits so they could gather. While Adriana slept in the curve of Tom's arm, Marcel snored softly on one of the wingback chairs. The fox snoozed comfortably on an arrangement of pillows in the corner.

Birdie's eyes had fluttered closed, though she struggled to keep them open as long as she could. Dodge cleared her throat, then cast her emerald eyes on Birdie. Her infuriatingly charming smile surfaced, warming Birdie's heart. "What is it now?" Birdie asked.

The smile turned to a grin. "I think we should stay."

"Stay where?"

Dodge pointed downward. "Here. I think we should stay here."

Birdie cocked an eyebrow at her. "At Willow Creek?" She laughed. "How many mimosas have you had exactly?"

"No, I'm serious." Dodge shuffled on the couch to better face Birdie. "We're safe now. And there's something special about this place, even after everything." She gently took Birdie's bandaged hands in hers. "Can't you feel it?"

Birdie smiled, a non-answer. Of course she felt it. But staying was a wild notion.

Dodge smiled back, released Birdie's hands, and settled onto the couch.

Birdie took another sip of her tea, her legs kicked up on the coffee table. She'd brushed Dodge's proposal off, and soon after, they'd fallen asleep.

The next morning, Birdie was amazed that they all slept so late. Now, as she soaked in the sun of that maturing new day, she couldn't deny the allure of the proposition. *Something* about Willow Creek did still pull at her, an imprint of home. Birdie belonged here.

She shook her head. It was a wild idea, impulsive. Dodge didn't actually mean it.

Did she?

The porch door clanged open and shut. "How's the sweet tea, palomita?"

Birdie lifted her cup toward Adriana. "Your best batch yet. Thank you."

Marcel joined them on the porch. "Are you sure you want to wait around for this vet? I'm sure the fox will be fine."

"I'm sure." Birdie set her tea down and hugged Marcel. "I'm going to miss you."

He waved a dismissive hand. "You better. Visit me the first chance you get."

She smirked and crossed her heart with her forefinger. "I promise. Where else am I going to get my fill of scandal and poetry?"

Marcel kissed her on the cheek, then gestured with his thumb at Adriana. "Tell her that. I'm still trying to convince her to let me do a reading at the opening of her restaurant."

Adriana scoffed. "I said maybe; I didn't say no. Putting the cart before the horse. I haven't even secured a location yet."

A car trunk slammed shut, and Tom jogged up the steps. He still had a pained look that hadn't entirely washed away, but when he was near Adriana, it dampened. "We're all set. Ready?"

Dodge came out of the mansion, laptop in hand,

donning her wide-brimmed black hat. "Not until you say goodbye to me, big guy."

"You're not leaving yet either?" Marcel asked.

Dodge winked at Birdie. "Nah, I'm gonna keep Birdie company while she waits."

Everyone exchanged hugs. Adriana squeezed Birdie tight. "Stay safe."

"Will do. Let me know about your restaurant and anything I can do to help."

Marcel and Tom retreated to the cars. Adriana lingered, then followed down the steps where she paused. "Actually, when you get a chance, pick a photo you took from here. We'll blow it up, hang it in the entryway. I don't ever want to forget our time here together. Not that I could!" She chuckled darkly, then grew serious. "What she did to us—we can rewrite that narrative—strengthen our friendship and use it to fuel the fires of our creativity. No one dictates our story, not even *esqueleto rojo*." Adriana blew a parting kiss before getting in the car.

Dodge hovered at Birdie's shoulder while they both watched as the cars disappeared down the willow-lined drive. They'd known each other for mere weeks, but the absence of Adriana, Tom, and Marcel tugged at Birdie's heart. Adriana was right. She'd finally found friends she wanted to nurture for the long haul, and the experience offered a solace she hadn't felt before.

Dodge tapped Birdie. "Come. I have something to show you."

While Dodge situated herself on the wicker loveseat and opened her laptop on the table, Birdie swung by to pat the fox on the head. She'd moved his makeshift bed outside only because he whined if he wasn't in the same room as her. He lapped water from a bowl she offered, his trusting eyes peering up, then rested his long snout on crossed paws. If she were honest, his company calmed her as well.

"Whatcha got—" Birdie plopped down on the plush cushion next to Dodge, speechless. Crimson blotches sprouted on her cheeks. "*Dodge...*" A warning issued through teeth set on edge. "What am I looking at?"

The Weeping Willow saturated the screen with its stunning jade-green leaves in mid-sway, restored to its full glory and grandeur as if the events of the past few days hadn't come to pass. The picture—Birdie's raw photograph—adorned the background of an online video. Underneath, the title read: "Dodge Dawson - Ninety-Nine Ashes."

"Before you get mad, just listen. Please." Dodge pressed play.

Her imperfectly perfect guitar strums punctuated the air. Birdie stood and went to the railing, leaning hard against it and staring at the flourishing lands before her. Dodge's chords laced around her heart, notes born of this place and time, full of scarlet clay and echoes of the dead. Around her, the desiccated flora reemerged, resilient and infused with new life.

Just as the vocals began, the recording abruptly stopped with a tap on the laptop. Birdie wanted to turn around, to express to Dodge how incomplete she felt being torn away from the track before it ended. But soft humming from Dodge continued the melody and halted her. Birdie waited, not daring to breathe.

Dodge sang.

"Witness,

O tree of willow weeping
Bound
By blood of passion, seeping

Foxes like banshees howl, they howl
Forewarned, the roots, they prowl, prowl
But ninety-nine ashes
From ninety-nine trees
Are not enough, no, never enough
Against you and me

Weak is the willow, tender is the hand
Clasped together, stronger, we stand
Bloom, singer, seer
Reject vile roots, together, you're freer"

After the musician finished her final refrain, the song imbued in the humidity buffeting their skin, Birdie gripped the porch rail, back to Dodge, and sighed. "You used my artwork without my permission."

"I did. I'm sorry." Dodge paused. "It's no excuse, but my fans are raving about the new song and cover art. I think I could really blow it out of the water. I think *we* could, together: your imagery, my music."

Birdie bit her lip. "Were you serious about staying?" She faced Dodge, crossing her arms, lower back resting against the wood.

Beams of light danced across the freckles on Dodge's cheeks and nose. She narrowed her eyes, unable to fully remove the hint of a smile. "Deadly."

Birdie searched Dodge's face and only found earnest determination. "All right." She shook her head and slapped her leg, moving to the steps down to the front lawn.

Dodge trailed after her. "All right? You're going to stay?"

Leading them to the path around the back of the mansion along the creek, Birdie spoke over her shoulder. "Yes. But there's one thing we've gotta do first."

36

Like a slumbering giant, the great tree lay broken across Willow Creek. Sunlight coaxed the rainy aftermath into the air, mist rising from the charred clay. Birdie and Dodge stood side by side in silence, staring at the ground.

Red-orange clay, unmarred by the fire, shimmered in an outline of what was once *esqueleto rojo*. Only no bones were to be found. Instead, rising out of the ground, impish and defiant, grew a tiny yet stout willow tree sapling.

Despite the heat dampening her brow, a tickle of ice skittered up Birdie's spine as if taunted by the unfurling, bright-green leaves of the burgeoning tree itself. Birdie slowly turned to Dodge.

Dodge locked eyes with Birdie, then marched off in the direction of the campsite.

"Where are you going?" Birdie fretted with interlaced fingers. "Dodge?" She worried. If Dodge was having trouble hearing, did that mean... Heart pounding, Birdie crouched to inspect the sapling. Against her better judgement, she reached to touch one of the leaves. She had to *know*.

The leaf twitched in her direction as a hand

clamped on her upper arm. Birdie jumped, stumbling backward. Sun radiated behind Dodge, axe resting on her shoulder, somber. She held out a hand to help Birdie up.

Birdie brushed dirt off as she gathered herself together. She clicked her tongue and wished she'd been wrong. But she'd learned not to ignore her intuition, not at Willow Creek. "I guess we have more than one reason to stay."

"That we do, love." Dodge tipped her hat to Birdie and offered the axe. "Care to do the honors?"

Handle secure in her grip, her wounds only dully aching underneath the thick bandaging, Birdie heaved the blade. While she worked, Dodge sang.

"But ninety-nine ashes
From ninety-nine trees
Are not enough, no, never enough
Against you and me"

THE END

The story doesn't have to end here! Spend more time with Birdie and Dodge in an exclusive bonus scene. Join Sara's reader's group and read the scene now at SaraCrocollSmith.com/WillowCreekBonus.

FREE SHORT STORY

You can't escape its grasp...

Concerned about her mother's unsettling phone calls, Samantha returns home from abroad to find the curtains drawn and the windows nailed shut.

Is dementia causing her mother's strange behavior or something much more sinister?

Claustrophobic humidity... creeping ivy... dark secrets...

Samantha's been the perfect daughter her entire life. As she uncovers what lies at the heart of her childhood home, she'll never be the same again.

Visit SaraCrocollSmith.com/Ivy to get the free short story "The Strangle of Ivy."

LEAVE A REVIEW

Did you enjoy *The Haunting of Willow Creek* and want more like it? Consider leaving a review!

Reviews greatly help other readers discover the book and let me as the author know you crave more hopeful horror stories. Even a sentence or two makes a huge difference.

Thank you so much, my spooky friend!

THE FASCINATING FOLKLORE OF WILLOW TREES

When researching to write this book, I delved deeply into the amazing history and lore surrounding weeping willows.

Enchanting tidbits like whispering winds, the secret keeping capacity of willows, and the prophetic powers of burning and consuming ninety-nine leaves from ninety-nine willow trees all make an appearance in the book in some form or another.

I also explored the elements of the trees themselves, using facts such as their widespread, invasive roots and lifespan to create unique interactions with the folklore elements. I even researched actual recipes that include willow bark so what Chef Adriana Martinez cooks up in the story was based in some truth!

Big shout out to Icy Sedgwick and her enormously helpful and insightful article "What Willow Folklore Surrounds This Beautiful Tree?" Also, thanks to *Garden Guides* and their "Myth of the Weeping Willow" article.

If you enjoyed this melding of nature and ghosts, you don't want to miss the free short story "The Strangle of Ivy" at **SaraCrocollSmith.com/Ivy.**

ALSO BY SARA CROCOLL SMITH

The Haunting of Orchard Hill: A Hopeful Horror Novel

Tell the bees I'm gone...

In the dead of night, Nina escapes her abusive husband with her baby son. She only gets as far as Orchard Hill when a swarm of bees forces her off the road and totals her car.

A mysterious old woman offers to give them room and board in exchange for help around her farmhouse. But Nina begins to suspect there's a dark past hidden in the creepy, desolated orchard.

Has Nina traded one nightmare only to enter another?

Ancient apple trees... eerie singing... tainted honey... her baby missing...

Nothing is as it seems at sunny Orchard Hill. As Nina

uncovers its terrifying secrets, she'll be pushed to her limits and come face to face with how far a mother will go to protect her son.

~

Love Letters to Poe, Volume I: A Toast to Edgar Allan Poe

An award-winning gothic anthology edited by Sara Crocoll Smith. Take a tour through Poe's Baltimore home, experience "The Tell-Tale Heart" through the old man's eyes, go corporate at Raven Corp., witness "The Fall of the House of Usher" from the perspective of a hidden Usher sibling, and much more.

ABOUT THE AUTHOR

Sara Crocoll Smith is the author of the ghostly gothic horror series *Hopeful Horror*. She's also the award-winning editor of *Love Letters to Poe*, a haven to celebrate the works of Edgar Allan Poe.

For an exclusive morsel of gothic ghosts and daylight horror, visit SaraCrocollSmith.com/Ivy to get the free short story "The Strangle of Ivy."

Sara wants to give a special shoutout to patron Brad DeMaagd, whose contributions helped make this book possible!

Made in the USA
Middletown, DE
06 December 2024